CREED

THE *Marquette* FAMILY BOOK ONE

D1293822

NATIONAL BESTSELLING AUTHOR

TRESSIE LOCKWOOD

AMIRA PRESS

CREED
The Marquette Family
Book One

Copyright © September 2014, Tressie Lockwood
Cover art designed by Clarissa Yeo © September 2014

Amira Press
Charlotte, NC
www.amirapress.com

CHAPTER ONE

Frowning, Creed rubbed his temples, but no amount of pressure could ease the pain. He guessed nothing would help, seeing he'd been up for the last twenty-four hours. Nothing in particular had happened in that time, but still, he felt the irritation rising, and it wouldn't ease until he dropped his head on a pillow and left the world of consciousness behind for a few hours.

Numbers ran through his head, which he hated. That was his brother Damen's area, but the bastard hadn't been returning his calls. Neither had his youngest brother, Stefan, been answering. Instinct told Creed the two of them were up to something they didn't want him to find out about. He swore as he heeled off his shoes and yanked his socks from his feet. Unbuttoning his shirt, he counted the number of times his brothers had done something stupid in the last few years, things that he had to go behind their backs to fix. At least once or twice a year, he surmised. His foul mood escalated.

Having shed all his clothing, he stepped into the shower and allowed water to rain down on his head. The cool temperature, though welcome, did nothing to ease his pain. He needed to dig through his baggage to find the pouch where he kept his personals. He'd gone back to living in a hotel, but this particular one wasn't so bad, and it wouldn't be too long until the renovations were done. He had thought a change at his house was what he needed. At least he could work in peace when he wasn't in the office and not have to deal with endless hammering. Now he'd begun to rethink the decision.

Too soon, he had to begin washing off or he wouldn't hear room service arrive with his meal. That might be another reason for the headache. When was the last time he'd eaten? Yesterday morning? He wasn't sure. The reports he had been studying took all his concentration, not to mention the countless phones calls. Many of them had nothing to do with Marquette Innovations, Inc., which also pissed him off. Newly added to the Forbes list of billionaires, he felt...what? He felt harassed. That's how he felt, damn them.

Creed stepped out of the shower and ran his hand over the fogged mirror. He stared into his face, noting the perpetual frown. A change was what he needed, yet he couldn't get out of his routine. MI had brought him satisfaction every time he walked through the doors at headquarters, but lately, it wasn't enough. Everyone jumped at his every whim, scrambling to please him. He had only to snap his fingers, and it was "What do you need, boss? Sure, boss, anything. I'm on it!"

He chuckled low under his breath and slammed a fist against the wall. Pain reverberated through his skull, and he leaned against the sink, waiting for it to pass. Who wouldn't want the life he lived? Who wouldn't give a limb to be so pampered? There was something missing, though—a challenge, he guessed. On top of that, he had begun to think now might be the time to produce an heir. He laughed again. How arrogant he sounded using the word *heir*. Still, that's what his children would be, heirs to the Marquette fortune. Creed and his brothers were overnight billionaires. Well, if one could call a decade overnight.

A knock sounded through the suite, and he groaned. He'd forgotten again. After running a towel over his wet skin, he wrapped it around his waist. He should have used the robe but left it in the closet. No matter. The hotel staff had seen more than a bare chest and legs in their time.

"Coming," he called and opened the door.

"Good afternoon, Mr. Marquette," came the sultry voice. "I'm Shada."

Creed met the bright brown eyes of a very beautiful woman. He stepped back to let her pass and enjoyed the view of heavy breasts beneath a boring uniform, curvy hips, probably thick, satisfying thighs under the skirt, and a nice round ass. His cock stirred as he followed her in, but he willed it to calm down. No need to offend the staff, especially when he wore only a towel.

"Right there is fine," Creed said as she rolled the cart into a convenient spot.

The woman spun to face him with a smile on very kissable lips. For some reason, she seemed overly excited, but he couldn't figure out why. Maybe this was her first time serving. He had visited the hotel countless times, even though he was born and raised in New York. In the beginning, he and his brothers came here when they could afford it, just for the luxury. Later, at various times, he had found the hotel's location more convenient to the office during all those late hours entertaining business guests. In all that time, he had never seen this mocha beauty, or he would have remembered.

Creed considered the smooth skin that looked so soft to the touch, the sexy lips, the wide eyes. She was fuller figured than any of his previous lovers, but only by a little. Skinny women had never appealed to him.

"I can tell you what we have, if you're ready?" she said.

Creed blinked at her. Maybe the bite in her tone had been a figment of his imagination.

The smile remained in place as she began uncovering the dishes. "We have your mushroom burger with aged New York cheddar and sautéed onions. To die for, right?"

Creed raised an eyebrow. "That's medium-well?"

She winked. "Of course. I don't know how you're going to eat all this, but you're a big man, so I'm sure you'll be fine."

"I think that will be enough," he said.

She went on as if he hadn't spoken. "Then we have watermelon, feta, and basil salad. And right here," she said, uncovering a smaller dish with a flourish, "you must try the orzo with wilted spinach and—"

"I didn't order that," he interrupted.

The foolish woman unwound his napkin from the silverware and stuck a fork in the concoction. "It's incredible. Give it a taste. I know you'll beg for it every time you come back."

Creed stared. What kind of unprofessional person had the hotel hired for room service? "I said—" he muttered, enunciating carefully.

"Come on. Just one bite, and I'm out of your hair to let you enjoy your meal."

Creed ground his teeth. The irritation that had settled just a little after his shower began to rise again. His head hurt, no less, and here was this sexy but annoying woman trying to get him to eat food he didn't order. Who cared if it tasted good? She needed to go away so he could wolf down his burger and get some shut-eye. He hadn't even intended to order the salad, but on the menu, it had sounded good. Now she wanted him to taste some pretentious wilted orzo or whatever she had called it.

"Like I said," he pushed between gritted teeth, "I didn't order it, so I don't want it."

A tweezed eyebrow rose in response to his suppressed anger. She didn't appear to be intimidated by his size or his temper. At least this was new. Most of the people he dealt with caved when he lost his temper. This woman was either too stupid to recognize the total loss of patience on his part, or she was very brave.

She picked up the dish and nestled it in the palm of her hand. Inviting lips and a deep cleavage offered him a treat. Resistance crumbled. Creed snatched the dish and fork from her fingers. A tingling began in his nose, but he paid it no mind as he aimed the utensil at her. "If it's not good…"

She chuckled, and he was struck by the prettiness of it. "Trust me, you won't regret giving it a try, if I do say so myself."

Her hands went to her hips as she watched him with eagerness. Once again, he let his dick direct his brain, and he stuffed a heaped forkful into his mouth. Regret was the least of his worries the second the food hit the back of his throat. His eyes watered, and the burning began right away. Creed coughed and choked. He stared unbelievingly down at the plate and then at the woman. The happy expression on her face transformed in an instant to suspicion and then anger.

"It's not that bad. You're kidding, right?"

Creed coughed again and shoved the plate at her. His throat was closing fast. Pulling air in became a chore, and his chest grew tighter. He opened his mouth to speak, but nothing more than a rasp came out. *Damn it! Nuts in my food? They've never…*

The full thought refused to form as he focused on getting air before he passed out. He charged toward the bed, but she stood in his path, hands on her hips, frowning at him. "Mr. Marquette, enough with the jokes. If you don't like it, just say so!"

Creed shoved her aside with one hand, and she stumbled, giving a small yelp. As she tried to right herself, her arm shot out to grab onto his. The stupid woman missed and caught his towel instead. She landed on her ass, and he rocked on unsteady feet above her—*naked.*

Through the fog that his mind was becoming, he saw her staring up at his cock, mouth open, eyes wide. He sank down to the floor, and his forehead hit her shoulder. As hard as he tried, he couldn't raise it. She shoved at him and managed to look into his face. At last, alarm registered on hers.

"Oh crap, you're serious! Are you allergic to nuts?" When he couldn't respond, she scrambled out from under him, knocking him sideways in the process. He went down hard. All he heard at that point were the ragged gasps as he struggled to pull in air through a pea-sized opening in his throat. He knew from experience it was a matter of time before he got no air at all.

"Where is it?" she shouted. "You've got an epi pen, don't you? Where?"

His luggage landed on the floor in front of him, and Shada scavenged for his pouch. She soon found it and popped the blue cap off the container, then rolled him over to push the pen against his thigh. Creed expected to have to help her in some way to realize she needed to hold the pen against his leg for ten seconds, but she did it on her own. In fact, as the lifesaving adrenaline passed into his system, Shada pulled the needle away and, with a hesitant hand, massaged the area. She had no doubt received some type of training to use it.

When he could breathe, Creed sat up.

Shada tossed the used pen away and hurried to move closer to him. She laid an arm across his shoulders. "Easy, Take it slowly."

She moved away, and he sucked in as deep a breath as he could and winced at his state of undress. How embarrassing and disgustingly weak for him to land in this mess in front of her. Sure, it was her fault, but that didn't make him feel better.

"Yes, I need an ambulance at…" Shada was saying into the desk phone.

Creed groaned. He staggered to his feet and fell against the bed.

"Wait, let me help you, Mr. Marquette," Shada called out. She slammed the phone down and rushed to him.

"I'm fine," he rasped.

"You might need another shot in a few minutes."

The paramedics wouldn't find him naked, damn it. Where the hell were his pants?

"Let me *help* you." Her voice was soft, full of fear. She seemed to know what he sought, even though he couldn't put his need into words or even gestures. Humiliation rose as she slid a pair of slacks over his feet.

"I…can…do…it." His heart pounded. He felt jittery, and his stupid hands wouldn't steady enough to grab the band of his pants. *Damn it, she's not even starting with my boxers!*

"Yeah, that's why you're speaking so well." She slid the pants up his legs and paused as she leaned over him, her face inches away from his. "Um, this part will be a challenge," she teased.

He concentrated on breathing. By some strange miracle, between the two of them, they got his pants on, and Creed cursed for the hundredth time when she grabbed the zipper on his slacks and slid it upward. All he could think about at that point was not getting his cock caught, but she managed to handle him fine.

By the time Shada straightened, a knock had sounded at the door. She ran to open it, and the room filled with paramedics, hotel security, and a man he assumed was the manager. Creed was strapped into a gurney, a mask for oxygen was slapped onto his face, and he was wheeled out of the room with questions flying at his head. He shut his eyes and breathed as deep as he could handle, but the truth was he felt like he was on crack. He hated the reaction from adrenaline almost as much as he hated the allergic reaction.

After being started on an IV drip and hooked up to monitors, Creed's equilibrium slowly returned. His heart calmed, and he began to feel a lot better. Allowing the hospital staff to do what they needed to for him, he lay still with his eyes closed. That didn't mean he was calm. He thought of the woman and what she had put him through. His anger surged higher while he relived again and again the humiliation he'd suffered.

Hours later, Creed sat on the side of the hospital bed, pulling a shirt over his head.

"Do you need anything else, Creed?" his assistant, Jeff, asked.

"No, I'm fine," he snapped. He didn't mean to, but Jeff was used to his moods anyway, and he didn't flinch. "I'm going back to the hotel, and I want a meeting with the head chef as soon as I get there. I want to know why the fuck they would give me food with nuts in it, knowing my allergy!"

"Of course." Jeff tucked the bag he had brought Creed a change of clothes in under his arm. "I can take care of it if you like."

"Hell, no! I want the satisfaction myself."

"Sure. Will there be anything else?"

Creed slipped his socks and shoes on and then stood up. At last he felt presentable to do battle. He charged toward the door. "Find out where my brothers are."

"You got it."

———

Creed ignored the outstretched hand of the man just entering the hotel manager's office. The white uniform and hat said he was the head chef, and the set to his shoulders and high chin said the man thought a lot of himself. Why shouldn't he? After all, this hotel was known for its quality and food. For that reason, and because of the way they had treated him up until now, he gave them his business. However, almost dying, incompetent staff, and lack of rest had changed his view.

"Mr. Marquette," the chef intoned, "you have my deepest apologies for—"

"I've been a guest here many times over the years," Creed interrupted, "and I was assured that you and all of your staff know of my severe peanut allergy. I can't even smell them without having a reaction. Yet I get food with them in it, food *I* didn't order?"

"Sir, I don't know how this happened..."

"It was my fault. I'm so sorry." Shada appeared in the doorway, twisting her fingers together, fear and sorrow in her expression. "I didn't know. I haven't been here that long, and usually I'm much more careful about this sort of thing."

He glared at her. Once again, his body's reaction took him by surprise, but memories of her helping him to get his pants on—*having to tuck me in!*—sickened him all over again.

"Ms. Howard," the chef growled, "what would you have to do with anything? I fixed Mr. Marquette's meal."

Creed gave him credit for taking responsibility.

Shada stepped closer and raised her chin. Creed thought he saw a tremor in her lips, but then it was gone. "I wanted... Well, never mind what I wanted, but I delivered his food and added a little something extra."

"Extra?" Now the chef's chest swelled. "Why would my creations need something extra! Who are you to add *extra?*"

Shada faced him. "I admit I was wrong. I'm so sorry this happened. Trust me when I say I know how serious a person being sick can be. I just wanted recognition for my spinach feta orzo, and I went about it the wrong way."

The chef sneered. "You wanted recognition? I'll tell you what. How about you find it somewhere else. You're fired!"

Shada gasped. "Fired? No, please don't do that. I'm sorry. I was wrong. Please, I need this job."

The man refused to hear her appeals. "I'll be lucky if he doesn't sue the hotel and I lose my own job. You think I'll risk my reputation for someone like you?"

Creed held up his hands, his anger fading just a little. "There's no need to—"

"Wait a minute. Hold on. Someone like me?" Shada stepped into her boss's face. "What are you trying to say?"

Creed cleared his throat.

The head chef's nostrils flared. "This." He gestured to Shada from head to toe. "This attitude. From the beginning, you've clashed with everybody. You're always angry and defensive."

"That's not true! Ask anybody. You're the one no one likes working for."

The man's face reddened. "Well, you don't have to worry about that anymore, do you? Don't expect a reference. Get your things and get out. In fact, I'm calling security to have you escorted from the premises."

"Enough," Creed bellowed, and both of them quieted down. Shada's eyes flashed as she looked at him, and she folded her arms beneath her heavy breasts. He looked away from them to the head chef, who appeared just as put out by his interruption. Creed's headache had eased after lying quiet in the hospital for a while. Now he felt a pulse beginning in his left temple again. "I don't want to be the cause of anyone getting fired unnecessarily. I won't be filing suit—*this* time."

The chef nodded, but Creed saw he hadn't changed his mind. Well, it had nothing further to do with him. He had received an apology and an explanation. Now, all he wanted was to get back to his room and sleep.

He left the two alone and started along the hallway toward the front of the hotel. When he turned a corner, he expected to end up at the bank of elevators, but somehow he'd gotten turned around. Grumbling, he retraced his steps, and his cell phone rang.

Creed stabbed the connect button. "Jeff, what is it?"

"I've found your brothers. They're in New Orleans."

"Why the hell would they be there?" He tried to recall if Damen or Stefan had said anything about where they were headed. Not that he kept tabs on them, but they did have responsibilities in the parent company.

"Um." Jeff hesitated. "Maybe you should talk to them about it?"

Creed clenched his jaw. He knew what that meant. His brothers had done something he wouldn't like. "Fine. Do you have a number? Because neither of them is answering their cell."

Jeff passed on the information and rang off. Creed continued down the hall and turned right. He still thought he headed in the wrong direction, because the passages were stark and boring here, while the area near the front lobby was more stylish, with landscapes on textured walls.

The next intersection emptied out into a locker room. A security guard stood with arms folded, watching Shada clearing her locker. Guilt stirred in Creed, but he assured himself she would find something else soon enough. He started to turn the way he came when he heard her speak.

"No, sis, it's okay," she said. "I've been through this before. Not a big deal." She tried to laugh, and Creed heard tears in her voice. He spun back to look at her, and she shifted the cell phone from one ear to the other. "I've got Lurch right here watching me. Like they have anything I want. Gotta go. I'll be home soon."

She disconnected the call and spun around at that moment. Her gaze lit on Creed, and she scrubbed an arm over her face. He found himself at a loss for words. He had made her cry.

Shada struck a saucy pose. "Come back to gloat?"

"Let's hurry up there," the guard said.

Creed silenced him with a glare and moved on impulse. He took his wallet out and removed a business card. "Call me. I'll help you find something else."

Her lips parted in surprise. "Why would you do that?"

"It was an accident, wasn't it?" He raised an eyebrow at her. "Or were you trying to kill me?"

A flash of guilt. "Of course not. Death isn't funny."

He wondered at the seriousness of her tone now and when she had mentioned sickness in the interview. He wondered, as he did then, if she knew firsthand what it was like, especially since she'd been so quick to respond and knew what to do when he had the reaction.

"Good," he said. "I'll expect to hear from you."

With that, he left her and found his way to the lobby and up to his room. Sleep called his name, and he intended to answer the summons until the next day.

CHAPTER TWO

amen, you've been avoiding me." Creed felt his nostrils flare in his anger. "What are you and Stefan up to?"

"Hey, bro," Damen said, and Creed winced.

"Don't."

Damen chuckled and sobered. "I'm here with Stefan, taking care of a little business."

"Here, as in New Orleans." The words weren't a question. Creed already knew from his assistant where his brothers had gotten off to. "I know Stefan likes to pretend I'm the sole owner of our company, but you at least I thought would be responsible. Damn it, Damen, when are you going to stop trying to be like him and accept that you're…" He found himself at a loss for words.

"A nerd?" his brother supplied.

"Don't be stereotypical."

"My IQ is one fifty-eight. I have a PhD I got for the hell of it, which I'm doing nothing with, by the way, and you're saying I should what exactly?"

Creed pinched the bridge of his nose. His head no longer hurt now that he had rested, but Damen's issues weren't what he wanted to deal with at this time of morning. Why did he always feed into it anyway? "I'm saying you're trying to break out of one stereotype into another."

"Now you're insulting our baby brother."

"Just tell me what the hell you're doing in New Orleans."

Damen hesitated, and Creed knew he wouldn't like it when he heard. That's why Jeff refused to give him the details and left it up to Creed to get it straight from his brothers. Noise from the background said Damen was in a crowded place, maybe a restaurant, as Creed could hear the clink of silver on plates and people laughing.

"Spill it, Damen. You know you always tell me anyway, and I end up having to wipe your asses."

"Fuck you, Creed," was the response.

"Well?" he insisted.

"We bought a restaurant."

"What do you mean?"

"Just what I said. Stefan and I bought a restaurant here in New Orleans. It's pretty cool, but it's not going so well."

Creed thought again of the background noise. His brother raised his voice at times to be heard over it. "Sounds pretty popular, from what I can hear."

"I'm not at Marquette's."

Creed froze. "You didn't just say…"

"Yeah, we named it Marquette's. There's a sign and everything. Stylish and classy, you know?"

Creed stood up and paced his office. He walked over to the door and glanced at Jeff with a look his assistant understood to mean he was not to be disturbed. Then he shut the door. When he returned to the conversation with his brother, he felt like he had better control of his temper. "We know nothing of running a restaurant, yet you two decided to give the place our name?"

"Jeez, Creed, get off it, will you? Listen, this is a great opportunity. It will be fun, something different than the corporate BS we've been dealing with for a while now. Think of it as an adventure."

Creed knew everything that Damen was saying was just a repeat of what he had heard from Stefan. Not that Damen didn't have his own thoughts. Damen was intelligent—the smartest out of the three of them. However, after Damen's wife left him, Creed had noticed a change in his brother. Damen had loved a woman who wasn't worthy of his time, let alone the Marquette name, and she tore him apart by walking out. She'd told him he was boring, and she couldn't stand another day in his presence. On top of it all, she had also left behind their daughter, Nita. Nita had been two at the time. As far as Creed was concerned, good riddance. Neither of them needed that woman. Damen seemed to feel differently, and when she showed up a few years later wanting visitation rights, Damen had given in to her.

Creed returned to his desk and dropped into his chair. He used a pen to tap the desk as a way to keep his temperament even. Placing his brother on speaker, he set down his cell phone and spun to the side to look out on the city of New York. This was another tactic to ease his mind. Sometimes the tricks worked, and sometimes nothing helped. Sometimes, he let loose a barrage of words he regretted later. At those times, he hated himself, because he never wanted to follow in his dad's footsteps. Not for any reason.

At last he spoke. "So I'm assuming you've purchased this restaurant for yourselves, just as a hobby?" He forced a smile even though his brother couldn't see it. "That shouldn't be a big deal. I mean we've got excess now, so much we don't know what to do with it. We busted our balls to get to this place, so why not? Right?"

"Yeah, that's right." Damen sounded more excited. "You're getting where we're coming from. I'm glad you understand. Oh, but it's not exactly a hobby. Stefan and I are serious about it. We want to do what we can to get it off the ground, but well, I guess we need your help. No matter how I crunch the numbers, I'm not seeing a way up."

Creed knew Damen. When he rambled, that meant he left out facts, and already Creed didn't like the "it's not exactly a hobby" part of his brother's speech.

"And since you're part owner," Damen went on, "I figure we need your input."

"Part owner?" Creed ground his teeth. "Tell me you didn't purchase this restaurant through the parent company."

"Why not? We need two signatures to buy. We had them."

"And you named it Marquette's?"

"I said I did. Creed, have you been sleeping enough?"

"Give me the numbers, Damen."

"I—"

"The numbers."

Damen ran down the profits and losses for the restaurant in the last quarter. The red staggered Creed, especially with Stefan, a man born for marketing, supposedly in charge.

"You're telling me you two have been at this for the last few months, and I never knew?"

"No way. We wouldn't do that, Creed, but we know how much of a stickler you can be sometimes."

"Thanks."

"The numbers are from the previous owner. The growth in the last month was some of what we did with Stefan's ideas. The reopening was great, but, well, now it's dying fast."

"You'd do better to sell."

"No!"

"Damen, don't be stubborn."

"No, Creed. We're not selling. Remember, we need two signatures."

Creed's temper flew out the window. He slammed a fist on his desk and heard the wood creak at the joints. "So you're saying you two are standing against me on this?"

"Come to New Orleans, Creed. I promise you. You won't regret it."

"I already do."

"Well, get the stick out of your ass and get down here."

Creed ran a hand over his face and sighed. "Tell me something, Damen."

"What's that?"

"If you own a restaurant—"

"*We* own it."

With his brother's words, he pictured the family name on a poor, dilapidated excuse for a restaurant, or worse, a *diner*. "If we own this place—"

"Marquette's."

Creed repeated the word with a sour taste in his mouth, hating that it was the same as their surname, which he protected like a beast because it was the only thing they could call their own growing up. "Sounds like you're at a pretty popular place. Why aren't you at the restaurant, having lunch?"

Damen uttered a shaky laugh. "Funny you should ask. We can talk about it later. I have to go. Later, bro."

Before Creed could say anything else, Damen disconnected the call. Creed was left to wonder just what his brothers had gotten him into. He stabbed the button on the desk phone that would connect him to Jeff and waited for his assistant to answer.

"What's up, boss?"

"Jeff, find out the going rate for restaurants in New Orleans. There should be paperwork filed here for one called Marquette's. I want it on my desk, ASAP, and get me a flight for…let's say Thursday."

"You got it."

"Oh, and Jeff?"

"Yes, boss?"

"Coffee, black and strong."

"On my way."

Creed turned to his computer and did a quick Internet search for local news in New Orleans. After a few clicks, he found what he was looking for. A food critic had written up a restaurant reopening not far from Bourbon and Royal Streets in the French Quarter. *"Charming ambience, amazing food, and a relaxing setting were the promised experience at Marquette's grand reopening, but did the eatery, originally established in the 1800s, live up to its vow?"* the article read. *"Ambience, yes, setting, meh, but food? Well, all this reporter can say is YAWN..."*

Creed read on to learn that, while supposedly skilled, the chef, a man who studied in the great Paris, had failed to please the eye—let alone the palette—with his creations. The critic questioned whether Marquette's chef had ever been outside of Louisiana and denounced the owners for forming such an obvious fabricated background for him.

Why should Creed be surprised? They had skimped on the chef, the most important element for a restaurant's success. Up until now, he had been the one to screen staff. His brothers gave their input, but their strengths lay elsewhere. Damen built the original website that brought them success, and he couldn't be bothered with anything that didn't have wires. That is, until he turned over a new leaf and became more social. Stefan had an artist's eye, which should have meant he insisted on the best presentation for the food. Whatever was happening down there, Creed needed to investigate.

He considered his contacts for replacing staff in a hurry and then thought of Shada. What was her full name? He didn't know if he had ever found out. Yet he had a clear picture of big brown eyes in his mind, and a curvy figure. He had failed to get the woman her job back, a fact he needed to remedy. She was a chef, he recalled, but he didn't know the particulars. That could be corrected quickly, and if she wasn't right for what he needed, well, he would think of something else on her behalf. A favor didn't amount to him inconveniencing himself or risking his business.

As he scrolled through the contact list on his phone, a sense of excitement came over him. What if he forgot about selling and helped his brothers make the restaurant a success? Could he do it? That aside, what would it be like to see Shada again when he wasn't naked and passing out? Now that the experience had passed, he could see the humor in it—and appreciate the view she presented. Yes, he definitely needed to see her again. Just to look. And then, after everything settled down, he would search around him for the perfect woman to have his heir.

Creed stepped from the taxi onto the very narrow Saint Louis Street and surveyed the property before him. The name "Marquette's Restaurant" was emblazoned in bold forest-green over the first-floor windows and door. On the second story were balconies protected by wrought-iron railings and accented with large hanging ferns. He appreciated in particular the old-fashioned street lamps at intervals and the signpost that displayed the menu. So far so good, he supposed.

"Creed, you're here!"

He glanced up to see his youngest brother in the doorway, a ready smile on his face. Creed's gaze ventured up to his brother's hair, and he smirked. The three of them were so alike in coloring and build, people often mistook them for triplets. Stefan managed to set himself apart with frosted tips at the top his of hair and by spiking it with gel or mousse.

"Hey," Creed said and shook his brother's hand.

Stefan drew him closer and slapped him on the back. "Come in. You'll love it."

Creed followed his brother. "Have you seen or heard from someone named Shada Howard?"

Stefan frowned in concentration. "I don't think so, but there's this new chef. He got here this morning, and, well, the other guy was pissed."

"I can't help that. I looked into his background and found he'd embellished his resume. That's putting it mildly. You know you two could have done that for yourselves."

Stefan charged ahead. "This is the main dining room. Would you get a load of the piano? A baby grand, and it's tuned. The music we send out of here brings them."

"But you can't keep them," Creed countered.

He glanced around, taking in the large room, and he had to admit his brothers had done a good job. The place had a certain elegance. But as he inspected the building, going from room to room, he also spotted some problems, places where it looked like they had rushed repairs to get to opening. He imagined all Stefan had dreamed of was the entertainment portion.

"This isn't ready for opening, Stefan."

His brother gaped at him. "But we've been open for a month."

He shook his head. "You called me down here for a reason, didn't you?"

The sheepish look he expected surfaced. "Yeah."

"Sorry, bud, but you don't open a restaurant in a month or even three. I did some reading on the plane, and I'm far from an expert, but I got a little idea. We need to get someone who knows what they're doing."

"No way."

"Stefan."

His youngest brother stood firm, and Creed tried to recall when Stefan and Damen stopped listening to him. Maybe back in high school, a long time ago.

"It's not that I want this to fail, Creed, but I think we're forgetting where we came from."

Creed frowned. "I know where we started."

"This is going to be hands-on, not delegated."

"We don't know—"

"We're going to learn."

Creed ground his teeth, but Stefan smiled, the grin lighting his emerald gaze. While Creed knew they all had those same eyes, he had always thought his youngest brother's were different. He had done everything in his power to make sure Stefan was happy. Both he and Damen did, all during their childhood.

"And if it crumbles around our ears?" Creed grumbled.

"Then we'll deal with it."

"I'm not going to allow anything to sully our name."

"Sounds good to me," Damen announced as he entered the second-floor room where they stood. Creed's middle brother shook his hand and left it at that. He didn't hug him as Stefan had. Creed took in the pressed dark slacks and the wrinkle-free sky-blue button-down shirt. Damen shoved black-rimmed glasses higher on his nose, his green eyes sparkling with suppressed excitement. *Yeah, he's not a nerd at all.*

They moved to the office, which would be shared among the three of them. This wasn't a problem, since the property was generous in all respects. Next, Creed inspected the kitchen. He sighed in relief to find it to be in the best shape of the entire restaurant. Updated appliances, new tile, ample storage, and best of all, a larder full of food greeted him.

Creed met the small staff in person for the first time, and the head chef. He shook the man's hand and noted the arrogant attitude. Maybe it came with the territory, but at least this one had potential. He had already met with him and even sampled a few of his creations. Creed still felt there was some dynamic he missed, but he couldn't put his finger on it.

"So what do you think, Creed?" Damen joined him as he reentered the office, and Stefan brought up the rear. "It's going to be good, isn't it? Now that we have your new chef?"

Creed pushed his hands into his pockets. "The floor in the main hall. It can't stay like that, Damen, and you know it. If someone were to catch their foot…"

Damen groaned. "You're right."

Creed glanced at Stefan. "*We* don't fix floors. Understood?"

Stefan caved. "Okay, we can get workmen in for that."

"And a few other things."

"But we'll stay and oversee it," Stefan insisted.

"Whatever." Creed saw the way his brother bounced on his heels and knew Stefan hadn't revealed all of his plan.

"How cool would it be to have the Marquettes serving?"

Creed stared. "Are you insane, Stefan?"

"Damen's already agreed."

"Bullied into it, more like," Damen said.

"I'm not serving tables." Creed folded his arms over his chest.

"I already have your uniform." Stefan winked, reminding Creed of someone else with the same overeager attitude.

"Do you want me serving fools, Stefan, and lose my temper?"

Both his brothers paled.

"We might be out of business in a week," Daman said.

Creed bristled.

"Okay, okay," Stefan conceded. "You can be the manager. Keep all of us on point. Oh, wait, you already do that. Boring."

Creed started to respond to this second dig at his personality and general usefulness, when they were interrupted.

"Hello, I called from the door, but no one answered." A young woman with long, flowing blond hair and beautiful blue eyes gave them a wave. "I'm supposed to start here today, waitressing."

Both Damen and Stefan darted forward to take her hand, and Creed took his time joining them. He did appreciate the beauty, but he switched his mind into work mode. Might as well get started and at least try to rein in his brothers while he was at it.

CHAPTER THREE

Shada held up a blouse and frowned at it. "Sis, are you sure about this one? I think it shrank in the wash the last time."

Her foster sister, Marisa, turned to examine the top. With tiny buttons that ran from the bottom hem to the top hem at the front, it had once been cute. The Victorian-style ruffles at the neck and the short bell sleeves always gave Marisa a look of having escaped from the past, and Shada loved the blouse on her.

"How can you tell?" Marisa asked. "It's a belly shirt."

"Yeah, but it shouldn't be so short your boobs hang out the bottom."

Marisa chuckled and then coughed, making Shada worry. Shada tried to keep her sister cheerful, but half the time she ended up regretting making Marisa laugh, especially when it turned into an exhausting coughing fit.

"Are you okay?" Shada dropped the blouse and rushed to her sister. She gently rubbed her back.

Marisa waved her off. "I'm fine. Stop worrying. I let you pack for me, didn't I?"

Shada smirked and rolled her eyes. "Yeah, you let me. I'm throwing this thing out. We can buy new clothes."

Marisa had gone back to her reading, but at Shada's words, she looked up with a frown. "We shouldn't spend the money we don't have too quickly. Let's wait until we get down there and get settled."

"Why does that sound like you expect me to get fired?"

"No way, Shada. Anyone who tastes the deliciousness of your food couldn't help but hire you. You even tried to kill Creed Marquette, and he still wants to employ you."

Shada burst out laughing. "Damn, do you have to rub it in? I feel like crap about it as it is. But, girl, you should have seen his—"

"Ah!" Marisa held up a hand, her pale cheeks going pink. "I dreamed about it the whole night after you told me. All I could imagine was...well, never mind. I don't need a repeat of it. No one but Shada Howard could have stripped a man naked and then saved his life."

"I didn't strip him. Although I could have, because he was yummy."

Marisa blinked at her. "I wonder what my book has to say about that."

"Don't you dare psychoanalyze me, Marisa. This was not some Freudian slip."

"Freud would disagree."

"I don't want to hear from him, and that's final." Shada

28

suppressed a grin and got back to packing Marisa's things. "I'm so excited! Can you imagine? He hired me as the chef at his restaurant? *Me?* It's a dream come true. I've always been fighting to get recognized, and one mistake gets me here. I call that fate, not Freud!"

Marisa smiled, but Shada noted the dark rings starting to form around her sister's eyes. She needed her rest, and Shada intended to insist she hit the sack earlier than usual because of their flight in the morning. A three-hour plane ride would wear Marisa out, even if she napped while they flew. Shada had made sure to take care of every detail, including having their things shipped down, unpacked, and placed in their new apartment before they arrived. Because he was offering a job in another state, Creed had given her an advance for relocation. Already, the man was shaping up to be a fantastic boss, better than all the others she'd had. They had embarrassing history, but if he could get past it, so could she. *I definitely will, for the salary he's offering.*

"New Orleans, Marisa," she chirped. "We're going to be living in the world-famous French Quarter. I can't wait!"

"Me either," Marisa agreed. Then she sighed. "Are you sure, Shada? You had just gotten that new job, and your boss liked you."

"Don't be negative, sis."

"I'm just saying it was a bird in hand."

"One I got for my butt."

Marisa blinked at her. Her sis knew nothing of having too much junk in the trunk or the temptations it could provide for the male population. Marisa had been rail-thin and sickly all her life. The diagnosis of cystic fibrosis came late, and the disease grew severe in adulthood. Her health aside, Marisa was a pretty redhead with no ass. Shada adored her just as she was.

"He liked my ass too much," Shada said. "Come to think of it, before all the crazy happened, I'm pretty sure Creed's gaze strayed to my boobs a few times."

Marisa seemed annoyed at her words. "Are you sure it's not all in your head? After all, your response to them looking is what gets you in trouble a lot of times."

Shada held up a finger to emphasize her point. "No, the fact that these men don't know how to keep their hands to themselves is what gets them slapped. Get it straight."

"And cursed out."

Shada rolled her eyes. "Whatever."

After they left the talk of men and jobs behind, Shada encouraged her sister to get into bed, and she took the rest of the items she needed to her own room to finish packing. Early the next day, a mover was coming to gather the items she had packed, and they were heading to the airport. She had elected to take a flight later than first thing, because Marisa needed a lot of extra time waking up and getting ready. Mentally, Shada went over all she needed to do regarding transferring Marisa to a new doctor and hospital for her regular care. Shada was pretty sure she had arranged everything and gotten the paperwork in order, but she liked to triple check.

As she taped the last box, Shada recalled the experience with Creed. Her stomach clenched at what had almost happened. The thought that she might have killed him still weighed on her mind. Entering foster care at thirteen because her parents were killed and then having Marisa become sick to the point of living on disability, Shada didn't take this type of thing lightly. Hell, she was trained in lifesaving techniques, for Pete's sake. She had been credits away from becoming a registered nurse when she realized her real passion and became a chef. Thanks to the ever-psychoanalyzing Ms. Marisa, who had accused her of becoming a nurse only out of a misguided sense of responsibility, she'd faced the truth of her real love—food.

Shada shook her head, smiling. She loved Marisa more than anyone, and she wouldn't go anywhere without her. Her sister had been willing to move at the drop of a hat, all because of Shada's excitement.

This will be fine, won't it? she wondered for the millionth time. Sure, she could be impulsive, and that's what had gotten her in trouble when her old boss refused to let her try some of her own dishes on the hotel guests. The move had been foolish, dangerous, and it could have landed her in serious hot water, beyond just getting fired. Why did she have to act without thinking sometimes? Tunnel vision was what Marisa called it, and a temper, anger that came from the feeling that so often life wasn't fair. Shada tended to fly in the face of it to forge her own way. So far, she had fallen flat on her face more often than not.

"This time it's going to be different," she muttered and caressed the job-offer letter from Creed. "I'm going to prove myself to him and the people of New Orleans. I'm the best damn chef out there!"

She chuckled and headed in to take a shower. Tomorrow was a big day and the beginning of a new life.

Shada stepped inside the restaurant and breathed in the atmosphere of the place. Jazz music played overhead. She had expected a sea of tables and chairs with pristine white tablecloths and fancy settings, all waiting for patrons. Instead, the tables were missing, and there were spots on the floor where someone had obviously been making repairs. A runway had been taped off to indicate where one could step safely. She navigated it, hearing voices in the back. When she reached double doors with round porthole-like windows, she knew she had arrived at her kitchen. She pushed her way inside. A thrill raced through her system at the sight of the gigantic commercial refrigerators, the stoves, the unbelievable counter space. She assumed the additional doors to her right led to the pantry and maybe a walk-in freezer. The hotel restaurant had been fancy, but Marquette's just felt better.

A man in glasses stood leaning against the counter, eating a plate of food. He spoke with another man, and Shada could have sworn they were twins. Big builds, dark hair. She couldn't see the color of their eyes, but something about them put her in mind of Creed.

"Hello," she called.

Both men stopped talking to face her. The one in glasses seemed to perk up. He set his plate down on the counter and scooted over to her. "Hello, you are...?"

He took her hand and held it, not even shaking it but trapping her in his grasp. The intensity in his gaze made her blink as he studied her face. Shada was aware of how sexy he was, and he smelled delicious, but physically, she didn't respond. This man seemed like a knock-off of Creed, and she almost laughed thinking about it.

"I'm Shada Howard. Are you Creed's brother?"

Before he could answer, the other man moved forward and knocked his brother away. "Don't mind him, Shada. That's Damen, and I'm Stefan. Yes, we're Creed's brothers. Welcome to New Orleans and Marquette's. Did you have a good flight down?"

She somehow retrieved her hand. So the middle brother was a flirt. Good to know. "Yes, it was great. Thanks. I can't believe how different this city feels from New York. I've never been anywhere, so this is exciting for me."

"Then I hope you'll come to love it as my brother and I have," Stefan said. "We've traveled many places around the world, but we found we haven't wanted to leave since we got here."

"Has nothing at all to do with the money pit, I guess."

All three of them spun around at the voice, and this time, Shada's heart seemed to jump into her throat. She hadn't seen him since he interviewed her. The entire process had been so fast, her head had spun and she'd accepted his offer before she knew it.

She studied Creed as he approached them from a section she hadn't noticed, with further passages and doorways. Offices and other storage rooms, she assumed. No, Creed and his brothers weren't twins, at least not the identical sort. The one with glasses had sharper features, a narrower jaw. The one with blond tips appeared softer but not unmanly. Creed had been cut from steel, his nose almost hawkish, as if he had broken it before. She imagined the firm lips formed into a frown more often than not, but they still made her want to kiss them.

When he drew up to her, his natural male scent, devoid of cologne, filled her nostrils. Had she thought a moment ago Damen smelled good? Creed overwhelmed her senses and weakened her knees. Her heart hammered to the point that she worried he and the others would notice.

Get a grip, Shada. He's your boss.

"Good to see you again, Creed. Thank you again for giving me this chance. I won't let you down."

"Likewise. I'm sure you won't."

A couple of other people entered the room, but Shada was so keyed up, she barely heard their names. No matter. She would learn who everyone was soon enough. Creed gave her the royal tour, and they ended it back in the kitchen. Someone had opened a window, and a breeze blew in. She caught the strains of funk music playing somewhere in the distance and the ding of a trolley.

"This place is incredible!" she blurted, and the others laughed. Feeling Creed's eyes on her, she spun toward the walk-in freezer and pulled it open. "Where do you keep the fresh foods?"

Creed joined her, passing too close behind. She thought she felt heat from his body. He gestured to the door next to the freezer. "Over here, there's plenty of storage, all compartmentalized. Canned goods and..."

She opened the door, and then wrinkled her nose, horror washing over her. "Wait, is that canned green beans? Are you kidding me? No way. Not happening. My kitchen isn't serving canned vegetables! I'll go through my selections for the menu and decide what I want and then write up a list for someone to do the shopping. There's got to be a grocer in the area that provides fresh produce."

Shada waited for an answer with her hands on her hips. When Creed had moved to show her the pantry, the others had fallen into conversation among themselves, but at her speech, everyone fell silent. She looked at their faces and noted a couple of pink cheeks. What had she said wrong?

"Uh, Shada—" Stefan began.

"My office," Creed interrupted and took her elbow to guide her from the kitchen. The tightness in his tone brooked no argument, and her stomach tied into knots. She followed him down a short hallway and into an office that looked like it was straight from the eighteen hundreds, except it included a big-screen Mac computer, a printer, and other modern equipment. Creed shut the door. "I think you have the wrong impression."

She glared at him. "If you want to run a restaurant that skimps on quality food, you're making a big mistake, Creed. This place is beautiful. You can see the history when you walk through the doors. If you serve crap, the customers will disappear. Please think about it."

He leaned on his desk and crossed one ankle over the other. "That's not the problem."

"Then what is? I—" She clamped her teeth together. "I'm doing it again, huh? Running my mouth, voicing my opinion and criticizing those in charge. I'm sorry. I tend to do that, always acting like... oh, never mind."

He gazed at her, and she wondered what ran through

his head. At least he didn't appear angry at her. "I don't mind you voicing your opinion."

"Just watch the way I say it?" She had trouble keeping the grin hidden, but Creed didn't smile back.

"No, say it any way you like."

Her eyes widened. "Are you serious?"

"Yes, I hired you knowing you're outspoken, Shada. Remember, I know firsthand."

She groaned. "Don't remind me. Our meeting wasn't a good first impression."

He coughed. "Let's not bring that up."

Shada almost laughed, realizing he didn't like remembering his weakness, but then she recalled what she'd had to do. Damn, this was the first day, and she had been intimate with her boss. Her fingertips had touched his cock as she tucked it inside his pants and zipped him up. She couldn't help it. He'd been so weak and shaking so hard. At the time, guilt, shame, and fear arrested her, but now that wasn't an excuse. Her pussy clenched at the thought that behind the slacks he wore today was a very perfect specimen of manhood.

Stop, stop stop! Get it out of your head, Shada!

"I'm sorry if my letter wasn't clear," Creed was saying.

She mentally shook herself to focus on his words. "What do you mean?"

"You're not the head chef at Marquette's, Shada. Rene is."

Shada stared at him. Her throat dried, and where her heart had been pounding because of the powerful attraction to Creed a moment ago, it seemed to have stopped now. "W-who is Rene?"

Then she recalled the man she had been introduced to, the tall, lanky man with stringy hair tied back in a ponytail. She remembered the snapping hazel eyes at her polite but distracted response to meeting him. In essence, this man, Rene, was her boss, with the power to fire her. She wasn't in charge of the kitchen. In fact, with everyone there, including Rene, she had declared what would and wouldn't happen regarding the menus.

Shada sagged against the door, her breathing becoming ragged. "Oh, goodness. I can't believe it. I'm so embarrassed." She bent over, whimpering.

Creed darted to her side and laid a hand on her back. "Breathe. It's not as bad as it seems."

He made it worse with his kindness. "It is!" She moved away from him. "I basically insulted my boss. Chefs are artists—they're notorious for being sensitive. I thought this was going to be a better experience, but here I am chewing my foot again!"

Amusement lit his gaze. "You'll recover."

"This isn't funny, Creed."

"Isn't it?"

She frowned at him. "Are you laughing at me as payback because of what happened before? That's real professional."

"Don't bring that up."

"No, because you didn't look too good then."

He stepped up to her, towering above her five-foot-four-inch height. "I looked my best, actually."

An image of him stark naked flashed in her mind. She had to agree but scrambled for a comeback. What the heck was she doing standing here arguing with him in the first place? Creed laughing at her had pissed her off, and she wanted to get him back. All she could think of was touching him again when he was well. The smirk on the arrogant bastard's face said he knew it too.

Shada retreated, but she bumped against the door. "I can't—"

"Can't what?"

She was going to say she couldn't work for him.

"I checked up on you before I made the job offer. You have limited experience, and at each of the jobs you've held previously, you clashed with staff because you don't know how to keep your mouth shut. I told you that's not a problem for me, but you can't work here because you're not in charge? This is a new venture for my brothers and myself. Why would I hire an inexperienced chef to run the kitchen?"

"You're right," Shada snapped. She knew he was, but she couldn't help being pissed at him for spelling it out. Why the hell was she even here? She spun to face the door and put a hand on the knob.

"Are you running away?"

She glared over her shoulder at him. "Excuse me?"

"This time you aren't fired. No one is suppressing your creativity."

"Give it time."

He raised his eyebrows. "So you'll walk away *before* you're screwed."

"I didn't say that." She faced him. "Why do you care?"

"I don't."

"Then why are you trying to get me to stay?"

"I need a sous chef. Period. You're either the woman for the job, or you're not. It's a simple matter, Shada. If you can't handle it, I'll find a replacement."

Shada wanted to call him all kinds of bastards and other, more colorful language to his face, but that might be going too far. He was cold as ice and direct. She should appreciate the fact that she knew where she stood.

"Oh, I can handle it all right." She stared him down, not allowing her gaze to shift away. All of a sudden, she became aware that he stood too close, but with the challenge he'd issued her, she couldn't move. Creed knew what he did to her, and he held her attention. Her chest tightened, and she licked her lips, trying to calm down. "I won't run away."

"Good." Had his voice always been that deep?

"And, um…" She paused.

"Was there something else?"

He never looked away from her face. Unmoved, he waited for her to speak, and she clenched a hand at her side, digging the nails into her palm.

"You're the only one that can let me go."

Surprised registered in his expression.

"*Please*. We both know I'll have some hurtles. Let's put it like that."

He chuckled. Creed had a nice laugh.

She shook her head to clear it of such thoughts. "If you make sure Rene can't fire me, we have a deal."

"A deal? Interesting. You're a very unorthodox woman, Shada."

She sagged against the door and ran a hand over her

face. "I know. Damn it, I don't have any cards, and here I am, making demands on day one. You probably think I'm crazy."

"Don't sell yourself short."

When his voice faded some, she looked up to find he'd moved to his desk with his back to her. She sighed in relief, and Creed dropped into his chair. "You have an Associates in business management, and you're newly graduated from the Culinary Institute of America Hyde Park. You were even close to becoming an RN at one time."

"I've done a lot in my thirty-three years. I guess it looks like I've been all over the place."

"Depends on how you look at it." He scrutinized her, and she danced from foot to foot, hating how he robbed her of peace. "Okay, you have a deal. Rene won't have the power to let you go. But make no mistake. I've fired many people in my time. I won't hesitate to make any decision I need to for the success of the restaurant."

She saluted and smiled. "Got it, boss. I won't let you down."

"Creed," he corrected.

She tilted her head and smirked. "Creed."

Her response appeared to startle him, but she couldn't read what he thought of it. Rather than prolong things, she took her leave and went to find Rene to apologize. Maybe the executive chef wouldn't hate her guts if she made up to him right away. Now that the shock of finding out she wasn't at the top of the kitchen staff had worn off, she realized she was better off anyway. As Creed had said, this was a new venture for him and his brothers. If its success depended on her, then that created a lot of pressure for her to produce results. She would do her best to support Rene, and she prayed he wasn't a dick. "I'll learn a lot from him and then steal some light to shine."

CHAPTER FOUR

Shada sat near the back of the group, one foot drawn up onto the folding chair. She listened to Creed explain the plans for the coming weeks. Some of them had already been implemented. He informed them all repairs had been done. She was glad. The scent of paint and plaster had begun to fade, and she was working with Rene every day to replace it with the delicious aromas of *chateaubriand* and *poulet aux champignons*. Okay, he hadn't exactly let her prepare the steak just yet, but he thrilled her when he used her *alciatore* sauce recipe. Everyone had raved about the sweet combo of pineapple and béarnaise recipe, one uniquely her own, and she got to enjoy watching them eat rather than being stuck in the kitchen the entire time.

The Marquette brothers might be rich as anything, but she learned fast that they were down to earth—Creed's lapses into arrogance aside. They seemed to get a kick out of laboring, with their sleeves rolled up, alongside their people. Every time she had spotted Creed with a paintbrush in his hand and paint in his dark locks, she'd come to a screeching halt and forgotten what she was supposed to be doing. Good thing his work didn't bring him to the kitchen too often, although when Shada cooked, she was lost to that secret world where she could let her imagination run wild.

"You know they're billionaires in their other life?" the blonde next to Shada whispered.

Shada glanced at Tiffany, a waitress with long hair and blue eyes. She was just the cutest thing possible, and she bubbled around the Marquettes, hanging on every word they said. "I've heard."

"And they're single," Tiffany continued, annoying Shada. "You can take your pick, because they're all hotties."

Shada blinked at her. "Me?" She hoped no one had noticed her fixation with Creed.

"Not *you*." Tiffany rolled her eyes and waved a hand. "I meant a person, a woman."

"Oh right, because I'm neither."

Tiffany looked at her, confused. Shada turned back to listen to Creed. Nothing stopped the blonde, though. "I bet being married to one of them, I'd never have to stand on my feet again. I'd have a maid to serve me in bed. I would never even come to this restaurant except to show off my clothes and jewelry."

Shada cringed.

Creed cleared his throat. "Is there something you want to share with all of us, Tiffany?"

The waitress flashed him a high-wattage smile, uncrossed shapely legs, and then re-crossed them. She sat up a bit straighter, pushing her boobs out farther. "No, I'm okay. I was just telling Shada I think this restaurant is so classy, and it's going to be a great success. I just know it."

"Thanks, Tiffany." Damen cut across Creed when he would have responded. "We couldn't do it without you."

She simpered. "Call me Tiff. Everyone does."

"Can we get back to the matter at hand?" Creed said, and both Damen and Tiffany quieted. "As I said, all repairs are done, and now I feel confident about scheduling the opening."

"A party," Stefan suggested.

"No," Creed snapped. "You already did a reopening only to close again. The public will think we're insane."

"Nothing wrong with another party, Creed," Damen put in. "The natives and tourists love it."

Shada listened as the three went back and forth, and she realized Creed didn't run the entire show. His brothers gave him a run for his money, but even while they disagreed, she was amazed at how close the three appeared. This was family, everybody depending on one another, making it happen together. A sense of melancholy came over her, and she glanced down at her hands.

"Shada."

She looked up. Creed stood in front of her. At some point the meeting had ended, and assistants from the kitchen were uncovering dishes of food. Even though the restaurant wasn't officially open, staff had to be fed, temporary ones and permanent alike, and the Marquettes were always generous.

Shada stood, and her thigh bumped Creed's. She darted away. "I should help serve."

He caught her arm. "Leave it a minute."

She waited but gave a small tug at her arm. He let go without fuss, but she felt him studying her face. Why did it always feel like he was looking back just as much as she looked at him? She didn't want to fool herself, and certainly she wasn't looking to bag one of them, like Tiffany was. All Shada desired in life was to cook and to take care of Marisa. Such a dream wasn't too much to ask.

"Tell me what you think of Rene," he said. "Specifically the food."

She gasped. "You know it's good. We've been throwing back for weeks now."

Creed grinned. "I like how you word it."

"It's true."

Creed checked to see if anyone was near. Shada noted the line forming at the tables. The buffet was just for now. Marquette's wouldn't have anything so common when the doors opened to the public.

"Is it *good*," he emphasized, "the food you've been practicing with him to make."

She grinned. "You mean is it alive? Will it capture people and not let them leave? I think it is. Rene's brilliant, but don't tell him I said so. He's not that social."

She rolled her eyes, and Creed chuckled.

"He gives orders, and we follow. Other than that, he's head bowed, fingers flying. I love watching him."

This time Creed frowned, and she wondered she she'd said wrong.

"I've decided to give you a dish for the menu."

She gaped. "Are you serious?"

"Yes. One dish, your choice. Rene has to approve it, the dish and the quality."

Shada bounced up and down, doing her best to suppress a squeal. "I can't believe it. Thank you so much. I have to look through my journal of recipes. Oh wow, what am I going to make? Chicken, beef, fish?"

"Whoa, slow down."

She put a hand to her chest and drew in a deep breath, then let it out. "You're amazing, Creed."

He started, and she bit her lip. "I mean—"

"I know what you mean."

He peered toward his brothers as they stood balancing plates at the baby grand while the performer plucked out an upbeat tune. Tiffany did her best to call attention to herself nearby, but Stefan focused on the music. Damen fielded a call on his cell and excused himself. Poor woman wasn't making any progress.

"The three of you are close," Shada said, not really questioning it.

"We are," he agreed. "We've come far."

"I bet."

"How is Marisa?"

Shada appreciated that he remembered. She had brought her sister by the restaurant only a couple of times, as the fumes from the paint and dust might have gotten to her. "Do you mind if I bring her by more often, now that everything's cleaned up? I don't like leaving her home alone for long hours."

He pushed his hands into his pockets. "Not at all. She's welcome anytime and as long as she likes. As a matter of fact, her meals are always free."

Something stirred in Shada. She lowered her lashes. "Thanks."

"Maybe you can let me do a taste test."

Her mouth fell open. "What?"

Amusement brightened his eyes. "Your new dish? What did you think I meant?"

"Nothing. I knew you were talking about my food."

"Hmm."

He excused himself and strode over to Stefan. Shada stared after him. The Marquette brothers were professional and kind to their employees, Damen a little warmer to the women, but Shada still felt Creed exuded sexuality. He didn't have to talk dirty or make innuendos for her panties to get wet. Yet more and more over the last couple of weeks, she had begun thinking the attraction wasn't just on her side. Unlike in his hotel room, Creed never allowed his eyes to stray from her face, but he seemed so aware of her.

Wishful thinking, Shada. Don't be like Tiffany.

She almost laughed at the thought. Marriage was not on her To Do list or even in her dreams. Sure, she had physical needs just like any other woman, but that wasn't the same as falling in love. Her heart remained under lock and key, and she couldn't say with certainty that it had ever been let loose—not for a man. Love meant pain. She loved Marisa because she couldn't help it, but her sister would be the last person she ever cared for.

A crash from the direction of the kitchen drew Shada's

attention, and she hurried to see what the matter was. Their *plongeur*, the porter or dishwasher, was leaning over the sink, panting, cheeks pink. A shattered plate lay on the floor.

"Sweetie, are you okay?" Shada touched his head. "You're burning up."

Creed and the rest of the staff strode into the kitchen.

"I think he's got a fever, Creed. He'll need to go home. We already have one *plongeur* out sick."

Creed swore. "I'll need to call an agency."

"Might be too late tonight," Stefan said.

Shada retied her apron. "I'll take over the dishes for tonight."

Creed eyed her. "I'll join you."

Tiffany popped up beside him and tugged at his arm. "Why should you do it, Creed? You're the big boss."

"We all pitch in. That's how we run things here." He managed to shake off her arm without appearing to do so. Shada gave him credit, but she didn't need the man working at her side, tempting her all night.

"I've got this, Creed. You don't have to help."

"Everyone else, handle the rest," Creed ordered. "You know what you need to do. I think it's best to end things where they are for tonight."

There were groans of protest, but soon, Shada found herself alone with Creed. She knew it wouldn't be long before Rene arranged to get the leftovers packaged for donation, but for now, she and Creed were by themselves. Her nerves were jangled, giving her trembling fingers. If she picked up a plate at that moment, she'd just do the same thing the dishwasher had done.

"Hey."

She looked into Creed's hot gaze. He stood too close.

"You don't hate working with me, do you?"

Her nerves untangled, and she chuckled. "The words form a question, but I heard disbelief in your tone. You think you're all that, Creed Marquette."

"Haven't you heard? I'm amazing."

"Don't use my words against me."

They both laughed, and Creed picked up the dish detergent liquid, then set it down. "Listen."

"Yes?"

He hesitated. "I'm careful about employer-employee relations. I know how things can get out of hand."

"If I've done—"

He held up a finger to her lips but didn't make contact. She fell silent. "Tell me if I'm wrong, and you'll never hear anything from me again. Nor will I ever behave inappropriately toward you."

Her throat dried. The nerves were back. "Wrong about?"

"About us wanting each other. In bed."

She had picked up a plate. Now she held it in a death grip. Creed reached over to gently remove it from her fingers. "I—"

The kitchen door swung open, and Rene appeared, carrying a pan of crabmeat-stuffed mushrooms topped with cheese and breadcrumbs. Shada had stuffed herself with a third of them. Behind Rene, Stefan made some droll comment that set Tiffany off in a peal of high-pitched laughter. Then the group returned to the dining room.

When the kitchen grew silent again, Shada released the

breath she held. Creed didn't push her. He waited in silence while she gathered her thoughts.

"I think…" Did she dare? He was basically saying he wanted to sleep with her, and hell yes, she wanted it. Still, getting involved with one's boss was usually a bad move. The whole thing ending in happily-ever-afters was a fairy tale. Not that she wanted such an outcome. She believed it could only lead to her being out of a job—again.

She started over after she took a second to calm down. "You aren't wrong, but I'm not sure we should pursue it."

Shada plugged the sink drain, ran water, and added dish detergent. Soon, she and Creed had a short assembly line going, and they worked in silence. Never in her life had she been so keenly aware of another human being. Creed's presence vibrated along her nerve endings as if he had invaded her body. She had to bite off a moan even thinking that way, because *invading her body* had all kinds of yummy overtones.

She washed a plate and handed it to Creed. He took it, and his sudsy fingers slid over hers, sending chills of delight racing along her spine. She pulled away, but he reached out and captured her fingers again. A gentle caress with his forefinger along hers made her shiver. He curved the digit over the tip of hers and traced under it to her palm. Moving up again, his fingers glided between hers and curled so that their hands were laced together.

The door opened. Laughter filled the air. Shada pulled back, but Creed held on. Their bodies blocked anyone from seeing what they did, but she felt exposed and vulnerable. Her pussy clenched with each touch, driving her crazy with need. He knew what the hell he was doing. The man hadn't taken her hesitation as an end to the discussion.

When everyone left the kitchen, she whispered, "Creed, you shouldn't do that."

He leaned down so his mouth hovered close to her ear. "I want to do a lot more."

"Like I said, I don't think it's a good idea."

"Pleasure between two people is always a good idea."

She made a rude noise. "Not if my job hangs in the balance."

He released her fingers, and she breathed a sigh of relief. The feeling didn't last long. Creed moved his damp hand to her belly, soaking her apron but lighting her body on fire. "I would never take your position away from you because we didn't mesh in bed."

"I don't know that."

"Then let me prove it to you."

She laid her hand over his, stilling his movements and keeping him from exploring lower. "You're making me wet."

Too late, she realized what she insinuated. He smirked.

"I mean—"

"I know what you mean."

His expression said he believed the dirtier interpretation of what she'd said. Frustration, desire, impatience at her own fear all battled within her. She didn't want to analyze this situation and figure out what was the right course. Not to mention she didn't want to follow logic if it turned out the best decision meant turning him down.

"Creed."

"Are you telling me no, Shada?"

Her voice trembled when she spoke. "Am I allowed to say no?"

"Of course." He moved his hand, and she could have wept. In relief and in disappointment. "I don't want you to do anything you don't want to do, because neither of us would enjoy it."

"I thought we already established I want it. I want *you*."

"True." He dried a dish and stacked it with the others he had finished. The sure and precise movements of his hands mesmerized her. What would those hands feel like touching her? Big, tanned, and veined, they could probably do a lot of damage if he was angry. Yet she saw tenderness there as well, sensed it when he laid his hand on her belly. His fingers could do things between her legs, she guessed. Shada shut her eyes to block out the view, but that brought her own imaginings into sharp focus. She blinked and studied the bubbles instead.

Does he moan during sex? Does he talk? Stop it, Shada!

"I don't want you to have regrets," he said, pulling her from her thoughts.

Together, they carried plates to the shelves where they were kept, and Creed took her hand to pull her into the pantry. He clicked the light on there and shut them in.

"This is too obvious," Shada protested.

"I'm stating my case."

"What case?"

She had hardly uttered the words before he dragged her to him with one arm around her waist, and he slanted his mouth over hers. Parting her lips automatically, Shada arched into him and brought her hands up to his chest. She tilted her head back and shut her eyes. His tongue tasted so good as it swept the interior of her mouth. Sucking on the tip sent sparks of aching need shooting through her system. Shada ran her hands down his sides and around to his back. She grabbed his ass and drew him closer. Just as she had hoped, Creed moaned, and his hold tightened. He crushed her to him and raised her off her feet. His cock, hard against her belly, slid lower as she rose, and he pushed the thickness between her legs.

When Creed set her on her feet and put her away from him, they were both panting. He held her shoulders in a firm grip, as if he battled between drawing her close again and pushing her farther away.

"There," he said. "Tell me how much more of that you want."

She tried for flippancy. "You're pretty sure of yourself."

"You told me you want me. Should I not have believed you?"

She grinned and shrugged.

"Besides, you've seen what I have to offer. I assume you liked what you saw."

All evidence of his embarrassment disappeared. He was right. She'd seen his cock and she'd been impressed, and it hadn't even been erect. Now with him swollen and thick, she longed to get a look—and a touch.

Shada opened her mouth to capitulate, but he spoke before she could. "I don't want to pressure you. You do this, great. You don't. That's great too."

Liar.

"However, let me make one thing clear."

She heard the note of warning and steeled herself.

"I'm not asking to date you."

Talk about a splash of cold water. "Excuse me?" She shouldn't be angry. After all, she didn't want a boyfriend either.

He rushed to explain. "Don't get me wrong, Shada. I'm not ashamed of you. Who my lover is, is my business. However, I don't want a girlfriend or even a mistress."

How did he go from being a considerate potential lover to this cold man who stood before her? Sure, in theory she agreed. She didn't want to get serious either, but just saying it the way he did pissed her off.

She moved past him and opened the door. They walked out to the kitchen, and Shada found his brother Damen there. While the man didn't say anything, a speculative light in his eyes said he'd noticed them shut away in the pantry together. She ignored him and finished off the dishes. Creed helped, but he said no more.

After she was done, Shada wiped her hands and said goodnight to the two of them. She had started for the door when Creed called out to her.

"I don't know, Creed," she said to the question he didn't speak out loud.

Damen peered from one to the other. "What are we talking about?"

Creed ignored his brother, and Shada spun away to leave the kitchen and the two of them behind.

CHAPTER FIVE

Shada stopped by the table where Marisa sat folding napkins. She'd only done four, although she had been at it for an hour. Laying a hand over Marisa's, Shada tilted her sister's chin up. "You look more tired than usual. Did you take your medicine?"

Marisa smacked her hand and smiled. "You know I did, commandant. You stood over me while I took them."

"Well, you wanted to come to Marquette's today, but I'm beginning to wonder."

Not more than a couple of years ago, Marisa had had a lung transplant. The doctors had a lot of hope for her once she passed the one-year mark, but she had good days and bad still, and it worried Shada to no end.

"Stop worrying," Marisa insisted.

Damen appeared out of nowhere and dropped into a

seat next to Marisa. Her sister's countenance brightened, and two spots of pink appeared on her cheeks. Shada frowned and narrowed her eyes at the two of them.

"I'll take care of the beautiful Marisa," Damen promised. He took Marisa's hand and kissed it. She blushed to the roots of her hair.

"Thanks, Damen." Marisa had the nerve to take the kiss in stride. "See, Shada? I'm okay."

"Leaving you with Damen is not my idea of being fine," Shada grumbled, and she debated snatching her sister's hand from Damen's and telling him to back off.

"Shada!"

She jumped and looked around.

Rene stuck his head out of the kitchen door. "I need you in here now."

"But…"

"Did you forget we're opening for dinner tonight, *cher*?"

Rene had been out of his head all morning, driving her up the wall. He was wound so tight, she thought he'd blow at any second, and it took all the patience she didn't have not to curse him out. The accent and the endearment didn't change that fact. The man didn't understand that she felt the same way. Tonight, her dish was on the menu, and everything that could go wrong had. The tomatoes weren't ripe enough, ruining her sauce. When she had sent a girl out to buy more, she'd come back with the wrong kind. In the end, Shada had had to shop herself, leaving Rene to have a meltdown about another issue.

"How could I forget?" she demanded and hurried to the kitchen. She would have to talk to Damen later about staying away from Marisa and to her sister about lecherous billionaires.

Okay, that was laying it on a little thick. After all, since she had avoided giving Creed a firm answer about sleeping with him, he had backed off. Not even a lingering glance had come her way. He was professional, and she would never suspect he desired her if she wasn't sure they had shared that kiss in the pantry by reliving it every bleeding night.

At last, the evening for opening to the public had arrived, and Shada peeked out from the kitchen to take in the impressive presence Creed and his brothers—with their broad shoulders and handsome faces—made in their dark suits. Shada overheard Creed's deep tones as he greeted two middle-aged women. The women tittered and fluttered hands at their chests as if they were schoolgirls. Creed had claimed to be bad at this sort of thing and refused to work out front, but for one night only, he'd said, he would play host. In Shada's opinion, the man was a natural. At least he was in charming women. He had them eating out of his hands with a few words.

"Another order for Shada's dish," Tiffany announced, entering the kitchen, and Shada rolled her eyes, hiding her glee.

"Oh, is that what we're calling it? Shada's dish? I'm a hit," she gushed.

Tiffany offered her a sour expression in answer. "Only because Creed is making suggestions to everybody that comes in."

Shada caught her breath. "Creed's suggesting me to the customers?"

Tiffany glared at her, lips pressed so tight they were deep rose, and swung away to deliver an order.

From then on, Shada worked with half her mind on the tasks at hand and the other half speculating on Creed's special treatment. She didn't dare deceive herself. Creed wouldn't risk the success of the restaurant if her food wasn't up to snuff, but neither did he have to push it forward to his guests.

"Compliments to the chef," Damen announced from the doorway, and Rene walked out to greet the customers who had called for him. Shada didn't mind a bit. She liked being in the back, creating. So far, she loved the position, and Rene was good to work with because he had taught her a lot in the short while they worked together. Nothing could be better.

"I said the chef," Damen repeated when he stuck his head in the kitchen again.

She frowned at him. "Rene already went out."

"The *other* chef too," he said.

Shada tried not to leave the floor as her spirit soared. Damen smirked when she passed him, and he patted her on the shoulder. Silverware clinked on dishes, the jazz musician and the piano player in the corner filled the air with soothing sounds, and the murmur of contented patrons at every table said the restaurant was a success so far. She paused and glanced across the room to locate Creed, and she found him standing at a table with Rene and an older couple. The air of importance the man gave off let her know he was a big shot, and she wiped her hands on her apron as she approached.

Creed gestured for her to stand beside him and placed a light hand at her back. "Sir, this is Shada Howard, and Shada, this is the mayor of our city and his lovely wife."

Shada's jaw almost hit the floor, but she caught it just in time. "How do you do?" Her voice came out raspy, and she cleared it.

The couple seemed gracious, and the mayor's wife took Shada's hand to hold it between her own. "That food—I told my husband we have to come back here again and again. I don't know if I want to try anything else. It was delicious, Shada. Thank you so much."

"No, thank you, ma'am," she said.

Creed spoke up. "You're both welcome at any time. I'll be glad to hold a table for you whenever you like."

The couple thanked them again, and Shada made her escape back to the kitchen. She'd scarcely closed the door and struggled to breathe when Creed appeared.

She grabbed his jacket sleeve, shaking. "The mayor, Creed?"

He chuckled. "That's a good thing."

"I know, but I've never met anybody that important. I thought I was going to fall through the floor."

He chuckled. "You'll get used to it."

She eyed him and recalled Creed and his brothers were pretty important people too. Maybe the mayor and others of high station came because of them. Creed must have met plenty of movers and shakers, so it seemed like old news. She began to wonder if it had ever been possible for the restaurant to fail, given who they were. No special grand reopening announcement had been needed, just as Creed had said.

After a few moments, she realized Creed was staring at her, and she looked up at him. He studied her face. "Are you pleased?"

"Uh, yeah! It's like a dream come true. Thank you."

In an instant, the cool detachment was gone, and she saw what she had seen in the storeroom a few nights ago. A thrill raced through her, and it had nothing to do with the food.

"Later," he promised and disappeared out the door before she could ask him to explain.

———

They served the last meal at eight-thirty and officially closed at nine. Even though Shada's feet hurt and she was tired, she was also keyed up. She stretched her arms over her head and worked out the kinks in her neck. They had their dishwashers tonight, so no double duty for her. Earlier, against her protests, Damen had run Marisa home and returned in a decent time, which told her he hadn't stayed to take advantage of her. She knew she was being overprotective, especially since Marisa had turned twenty-eight three months ago, but one couldn't be too careful with a man like Damen. He was nice, but he also didn't come off as serious. Shada wouldn't have her sister used, and she'd snip his balls off if he hurt Marisa.

"Shada," Creed called from down the hall. She snapped out of her reverie to go see what he wanted. Expecting to find he wanted to review something with her about her performance, she gasped when he tugged her into his office, slammed the door, and trapped her against it.

"Creed, what's going on?" She swallowed, avoiding his eyes, but his Adam's apple, the thick column of his neck, and the broad shoulders weren't much better. "You· said you wouldn't push."

He tilted her chin higher, forcing her to meet his gaze. "*If* you told me to back off. You didn't tell me, Shada. In fact, you've said nothing."

"Well, I was thinking." She wriggled to get free, but her thigh brushed his, and she froze. "I have cleanup duty. Everyone's going to think I'm shirking my responsibilities."

"Let them wait."

She realized from the glint in his gaze and the firmness of his jaw that he was just as keyed up after the success of the night as she was. The difference was, Creed's assertive personality came to the forefront even more because of it.

"I want you," he reiterated. He leaned down and kissed her throat. Her pulse raced. "In point of fact, I want to eat you up."

"C-Creed." Her body was on fire. She licked her lips.

Creed narrowed his eyes and pulled on the strings of her apron. The material loosened around her waist. He flattened the palm of his hand on her belly. "Do you know where I want to put my hand right now, Shada?"

"No," she lied.

"Should I show you?" he said, his voice low.

"Um."

Somehow she spun away from him and grabbed for the doorknob. He covered her hand and moved closer. Now she realized he'd let her turn on purpose so he could

63

spoon her ass. All of her willpower worked to keep her from grinding into him.

"S-so let me get this straight." *Damn it all, I'm over the stuttering. You're not a virgin, Shada. Stop acting like one.* "I want to be clear, Creed."

He nuzzled her nape. "Of course."

"If I say no right now and mean it…?"

"Baby," he groaned in her ear. Her panties were done for. "Don't say no."

She shut her eyes and rested her forehead on the door.

Creed pounded the wall with his fist, and then his body was no longer pressed against hers. She peeked over her shoulder. He had stepped back, his fist pressed to the bridge of his nose. "Go," he said.

"You're letting me?" She hesitated to move.

"I said I won't force you. Go now. *Please.*"

Shada pivoted in degrees. She eyed his crotch and saw the tent there. He reached his desk and leaned over it. The tension in his hand when he gripped the desk turned his knuckles white. This man wanted her bad. *Really* bad. The knowledge boggled her mind. He could surely have any woman he wanted. Hell, half the women who had come to the restaurant would have said yes if he'd propositioned them—no matter their age. Since she'd met him, he could have satisfied his lust many times, but over the last few weeks, she hadn't seen Creed leave the restaurant except late at night. He always returned early in the morning and worked straight through. This man had denied himself physical pleasure with a woman, as far as she could tell, and he had chosen her. He wasn't offering what she didn't crave, and he definitely wouldn't interfere with her personal decision not to fall in love. Nothing could be more perfect.

She walked over to him and rubbed her hand over his cock, squeezed it, and pressed her body to his. Chin raised, she challenged him with a look and waited.

Creed's arm shot out, and he crushed her to his chest. "You better be serious, Shada."

She kissed him and caught his bottom lip between her teeth. A tiny lick at it with the tip of her tongue made him moan. "I'm serious, as long as it's your place and not mine."

"Let's go!"

She pushed at his chest. "I have to clean up first. You'll have to wait."

"I'm the boss, and I say—"

"Wait for me, Creed. I'm worth it." *Check me out, getting all bold.* She spun away from him, ground her ass into his crotch, and walked to the door. At first she thought he would force her back, but he let her go. When she glanced over her shoulder, she saw a lust burning so hot in his eyes that she almost went back and begged him to take her right there.

Somehow, she made it through work, and then they were off. The last things Shada saw at Marquette's were Tiffany's scowl of jealousy and Damen's knowing smirk. Stefan had disappeared altogether, and Rene had walked off down the street in silence.

"I think they know," Shada said, sitting across from Creed in his car. She kicked off her shoes and rubbed a foot.

He glanced at her and then focused back on the road. "Do you care?"

"Sounds like you don't."

"Like I said, my lover is my business."

"We're not exactly lovers. This is a one-time thing."

"And if I want more?"

"Whoa. Wait, didn't you say we're not going for a relationship?" She held up her hands as butterflies fluttered in her belly. "I'm not in the market for a boyfriend right now."

"That surprises me."

She frowned. "Why's that?"

He shrugged and reached across to touch her lips with a fingertip. The man had an obsession with her mouth. Not that she minded.

"Something about you. But you're right. I don't want permanent attachments other than what I've planned for."

"Planned for?"

"Never mind. I'm not asking you to stay with me, Shada. I want your body. You're very beautiful."

She smiled and lowered her lashes. "Thanks. You're not so bad yourself."

"Plus you owe me."

"Excuse me?"

"I get to see that luscious body naked. You'll stand before me so I can have my fill of looking at you."

"Oh, I will, will I?"

"Definitely." He reached out again, but this time, he flicked her nipple through her blouse. The tiny peak pebbled at his touch, and she squeezed her legs together. She didn't like the knowing expression on his face and told him so. But no matter how much sarcasm dripped from her

66

lips and how much she teased him about the last time she saw him naked, Creed's amusement only increased.

"You don't care what I say, do you?" she demanded.

"Baby, all I want you to say to me is yes. And you *will* say it, all night."

CHAPTER SIX

Shada had expected Creed to take her to a hotel, especially with him just as new to the city as she was. When they pulled up to the house on about three acres of land, she blinked in surprise. The two-story stone-exterior house wasn't exactly a mansion, but the quality of the structure, with a wrought-iron fence that opened with a remote, came through loud and clear.

"You moved fast," she commented, but Creed said nothing as they drew to a stop in the wide driveway.

She followed him inside and paused in the foyer, gasping at the marble floors, the winding staircase, and the high archways leading off into various rooms. Was it lame for her to gawk? She wasn't sure, but her mouth fell open and her eyes widened all the same. This was how the rich lived, or maybe it was the way they slummed. The house probably didn't have more than four bedrooms or so, when she had imagined Creed's house to have no less than ten.

She glanced over at him as he shut the front door. "This place is—"

Creed lay a hand at her nape and slid it around to her throat. He moved up close behind her and pushed the other hand between her legs. A rough squeeze had her moaning and her lashes fluttering downward.

His deep voice sounded in her ear. "Forget the house."

He devoured her mouth in a hungry kiss and thrust his tongue inside to steal her breath. Through her pants, he rubbed at her clit until it swelled toward his finger.

Somehow she managed to free her mouth and turned her head. "C-Creed, I have to call home."

He released her with reluctance. She fumbled in her purse for her cell phone. Talk about aggressive—the man was ready to eat her up just like he said he would, and she was all for it. Why she had thought Creed to be a gentle man, she didn't know. Sure, she'd seen his kindness, but he was strong, and he often fought a temper. Right now, she thought he might tear off her clothes if she didn't get naked fast enough. Just the idea made her wetter.

"Hey, Marisa," she said when her sister answered. "It's me, sweetie. I'm going to be a little late tonight."

As she spoke, she watched Creed walk to the hall table and remove the keys from his pocket. He tossed them on the table and pivoted to face her. In one long stride, he reached her side again, nabbed the phone from her fingers, and spoke into it.

"Marisa? Creed. Are you okay?" he asked. "Need anything?"

"I'm fine, thanks," Shada heard her sister say.

"Good. She'll see you in the morning," Creed said. He tapped the disconnect button just as Shada was about to protest and tossed the phone beside the keys.

Shada frowned and put her hands on her hips. "Seriously, Creed, I could have talked to her. You didn't need to handle it."

He backed her up until she bumped the door, and he pressed a leg between hers. When he raised it, his hard thigh brushed her pussy, and she caught her bottom lip with her teeth. Creed lowered his mouth to hers and kissed her silly. He raised his head but didn't move far. "When I say I want to be inside you now," he whispered against her lips, "I mean it."

"Creed."

He snapped the button off her pants with one hand and lowered the zipper. Her gasp turned into a groan when he reached inside her pants, past her panties, and skimmed her clit. Creed's impatience didn't allow him to stay there long. He pushed lower until he parted her folds and eased fingers inside her pussy. Shada cried out. She grabbed onto his shoulders and dropped her forehead against his chest.

"Creed," she begged, but he ignored her desperate pleas as he stroked his fingers in and out of her pussy. "Fuck it, I'm going to come!"

"Yes, you are, right now." His command didn't depend on him ordering her around, but he raised her off her feet and held her against him. The man's strength knew no bounds as he held her up while he worked her pussy. She writhed and screamed, wishing she could arch into his thrust. Creed controlled all her movements while bringing her to the edge of sanity.

"Look at me," he said.

Confused, she struggled, and Creed stilled the movements of his hand.

"No, don't stop," she begged.

"Look at me, Shada. Keep your eyes open while you come."

"I can't. I've never been able to do that."

She put her head on his shoulder and peered at him through heavy lids. Creed licked her lower lip, and she mewled and shut her eyes. He withdrew.

"What are you doing?"

He raised an eyebrow. "I told you to watch while I bring you to orgasm. It gets me off."

"You mean you're a control freak."

He squeezed her pussy hard, his fingers moist with her come. She squirmed in his hold, but he didn't let her loose. Arching into his touch, she managed to get his fingers to sink into her heat, but Creed took them away again.

"Okay, okay, whatever you want," she said. "Just let me come."

"You'll come, as much as you want."

She nodded, and he pulled his hand out of her pants. With swift movements, he shed her clothing. Not even pausing to be careful, he yanked her pants down her legs and ripped her panties to scraps. She followed suit and tore at her blouse. Tomorrow, she might regret ripping one of the blouses she wore to work, but who the hell cared right now?

When she wore not a stitch of clothing, Creed picked her up, a hand at either hip, and all but tossed her over his shoulder. They wound up in the living room, and she landed on her back on the couch, with Creed kneeling between her legs. He lapped at her juices as if he had tasted nothing better. Her orgasm rose toward the surface again. This time, she cupped his head in both hands and pushed up to his face, groaning and encouraging him to feast on her.

Creed wiggled his tongue as deep as he could get it into her wetness. He moaned, sending vibrations through her. When he raised one of her legs, squeezing the back of her thigh, and nibbled at her pussy lips, she shouted his name.

Creed moved like lightning. He climbed up her body and replaced his mouth with his fingers. He massaged her clit with the pad of a thumb. Shada knew what he wanted. She gripped his arms and stared back at him. The lust, the intensity, his ragged breathing, and most of all, the feel of him playing with her clit, drove her to the place she longed to be. Her orgasm roared through her body, pulsing from her core out to her thighs and belly, seemingly all over. She had never felt one this strong, and she screamed.

Creed covered her mouth with his. He tasted of her essence, and he held her chin, hungrily kissing her. While he crushed her beneath his weight, making her feel small and feminine, he took her hand and guided it to his pants front. His cock twitched in her fingers, and Creed made her press hard. He grunted and broke their kiss.

"Where are you going?" she teased.

He leaned up far enough to tear off his shirt. She drank in the sight of his big chest and tanned skin, the narrow waist, and those hard thighs. Narrowing her eyes, she waited with impatience until he showed her the treasure she had seen once before and couldn't get out of her head. Creed hopped off the couch to kick his pants and boxers away. Shada reached for his cock, so thick and long. She curled her fingers around it and would have taken it into her mouth, but he pushed her back.

"No."

"But I know you like it. What man doesn't?"

"I'm coming inside you, not in your mouth."

She gaped. "Um…"

"I don't mean it like that." He found a condom in his wallet and snapped it on with impatient fingers. Creed sat down on the couch and drew her onto his lap, facing him. "Are you ready?"

"You can't imagine how much."

He raised her up but only allowed the tip of his cock to pierce her. She tried to drop down, but she was no match for his strength or control.

"Creed!"

"Look at me."

She did.

"I'm going to fuck you hard. Do you have a problem with that?"

If she did, would he not do it? No sense finding out right now, because she wanted it so much, as hard and rough as she could stand it. Her previous lovers except for one had been too soft, too hesitant, and frankly unable to keeping it going as long as she liked. Would Creed be different? From the little she had experienced so far, something told her he would.

Still, he hesitated. "You'll say dragon if you want me to stop."

She blinked. "Dragon?"

"Yes, because you will scream my name." He tangled his fingers in her hair and gave a small tug. Her head went back, and he nipped the skin at the base of her throat. "I'm going to go rough and fast. Even after I come, I tend to stay hard for a while, and my need stays strong. If you can take it, I'll make you come as many times as you want."

Shada laid her hands on his shoulders. "Dragon. I got it. I'm ready for everything you've got to give me."

Creed brought her down on his cock. Eyes closed, head back, she clenched her teeth as he sank deep into her pussy. Every inch fit inside, but his thickness stretched her walls so good. She murmured her pleasure and ground her hips against him. He hissed between his teeth. When they were one, Creed took her in a firm grip on either side and arched his hips until his cock slid out a short way. Then he slammed it deep. Startled, she cried out, thinking he'd go too far and hurt her.

The man knew what he was doing.

He wound an arm about her waist and pounded up into her pussy. She screamed his name, holding on, pleading for him not to stop. Their bodies crashed together again and again. She heard the slick, wet sounds of her juices coating his cock each time he slid in, and it drove her lust higher.

Creed's thrusts were fast, but they were nothing she couldn't handle. He loosened his hold and let her lean back. Her lover buried his face between her breasts. He kissed the hot skin in the valley between her peaks and moved to a nipple. Her pussy clenched at the first sting of him sucking so hard. She reached between them and stroked her clit with expert fingers. Creed switched to the other nipple, and she whimpered as another orgasm began to build.

He popped her off his lap and set her on her knees. A swift smack to her ass cheek had her moaning, and he rubbed away the sting. "Arch your back," he ordered.

She did, and he smacked her ass again. How she loved to be spanked. "Yes!"

"Deeper," he demanded. "I want that pussy open to me. I want to see your come dripping down."

She stretched forward a bit, like a happy little kitten, and pushed her ass in the air. Creed grasped her hips and plugged her pussy full of his shaft. Her mind spun. She couldn't get enough. He jerked her backward and aligned his thighs with hers. Slowly, he began a pump into her heat, as if he judged how deep to go. His pace increased a little at a time. After a few moments, he began to pound into her. She thrilled at the sound of their bodies slapping together, his grunts, and the slight ache caused by his invasion. Her senses went wild. The pleasure of him pumping so hard drove her straight to another orgasm.

Creed leaned over her back, kissed her, and nibbled her skin. He licked until she trembled. Just the feel of him curved along her body made her want to mewl. He flattened a hand on her belly, and she felt him jerk and moan. The curse he bit off between clenched teeth told her he was ready to reach his release, but he pulled out.

"Creed?"

"Turn over, Shada."

She did and lay on her back. Creed raised her legs and dragged her to him. He ground his cock into her pussy until she was filled to capacity. A few quick pumps, and he held her chin in place, leaned over her, and met her gaze. Shada stared into his eyes. The green of his irises darkened.

"Shada, your pussy feels so good. I'm going to come in you."

"Yes! Do it, Creed. I want all of you."

He came, his hips jerking, his mouth seeking, and his hands squeezing her breasts. When he was done, he slid his cock free of her and stood up. Sore, Shada started to sit up, but Creed raised her into his arms.

"What are you doing, Creed?" She protested and tried to get down, but his hold tightened, and he walked out of the living room with her. He didn't let her go until he had dumped her in his bed and joined her. Creed had covered his bed with pristine white sheets and a matching white comforter. The A/C blasted, chilling the air, so she loved snuggling beneath the covers.

He nuzzled her from behind but then moved away, and she heard the snap of the condom coming off. A drawer opened, and a package rattled. This man's sex drive was unbelievable. A thrill raced through Shada's body.

She peered over her shoulder at him. "You want it again?"

He reached for her and drew her back to his chest, a hand snaking around her waist. "You have no idea."

CHAPTER SEVEN

Shada checked her phone. No calls. She started to dial Marisa's number but then remembered her sister wouldn't be up at this time. Shada shouldn't have risen either, after the night she had with Creed. Every muscle hurt, and her pussy needed vacation time. She'd loved every minute of sex with Creed, though. How did that man even learn how to pleasure a woman the way he had her? Or was it that they were a good match? He went wild in bed. He became so authoritative. She loved how he had given her a safe word even though she found no need to use it. No one had ever done that before, because they had never taken her hard enough. She had always wanted it that way, but every time she had risked telling a lover what she wanted, she was doomed to disappointment. Not only did Creed like it rough too, he exceled at making her feel good and giving her just enough pain to give her multiple orgasms.

Now, with the sun just peeking over the horizon, she was starving. She didn't have her car, so she couldn't leave, and she had no idea what Creed's address was to call a taxi. As she saw it, he owed her breakfast, and she was going to collect on her own.

She laughed at her reasoning as she located the kitchen and found a modern layout that looked like something straight from a magazine. Forget the house, he'd said. She could only dream of having something this nice. The stainless-steel double-door refrigerator beckoned, and she crossed the kitchen to see what Creed had to offer. With any luck, he wasn't the kind of bachelor who had nothing but sour milk and moldy bread in there.

To Shada's delight, she found the fridge stocked, and she removed peppers, onions, eggs, cheese, sausage, and rolls from the freezer side. After she got the stove on the island going, frying the sausage, she started on chopping the veggies. Creed strode in just as she slid the pan of rolls into the oven. "I hope it's okay that I'm cooking. I'm hungry."

His hair stood up all over his head. She'd never seen him look so sexy. "It's fine." Creed's gaze lowered to her breasts and then her legs. "Is that my shirt?"

"Well, you did tear my clothes off."

"I think you were the one who popped your buttons."

"Whatever. I couldn't come down here naked."

"I don't mind." He reached for her, but she smacked his hand.

"I'm cooking. Don't bother me."

He grunted.

Shada prepared two plates of food. "Do you want some?"

He smirked and took a seat on one of the stools at the end of the island. He had dressed in a pair of shorts, and from the way his cock was being defined by the fabric, she guessed he had bypassed boxers. Being shirtless, he gave her an enjoyable view of his chest and abs. No man was built as perfectly.

Creed grabbed a roll when they came out of the oven, and she tried to smack his hand. He caught her wrist and dragged her to him. He kissed her lips and then bit into the roll. "I like honey on it."

His gaze traveled over her form, and Shada smirked. "Are you talking about the roll or me?"

A light danced in his gaze. "I might like to try both."

"Down, boy. I told you I'm hungry. I will fight you for food."

He laughed and spanked her ass as she escaped his hold to return to the meal. When they sat down to eat, she studied him, waiting for his reaction to her cooking. His deep moans had her recalling their pleasure from the night before. Creed ate with relish and heaped loads of eggs onto his plate. He cleared half the pan of biscuits, all of them covered with honey.

"How the heck do you stay in shape, eating like that?" she demanded.

"A little of what we did last night."

"A little," she repeated.

He stuck his finger in a bit of honey and held it to her lips. She grabbed a napkin and cleaned his finger, then laughed at his disappointment.

"I wanted you to suck it."

"I know. Maybe next time."

Amusement brightened his eyes and curved his lips. Damn, he was sexy. To distract herself, she picked up the last piece of sausage and bit into it. Creed watched her chewing, a look of interest on his face. Where were they going with this? Would they have sex again, or was last night a one-night stand, so to speak? If she knew what was good for her, she'd let it become a great memory and leave it there.

"So I read this short piece on you in Forbes magazine," she began.

"Hmm."

"It said you and your brothers were from humble beginnings, but it didn't really go into any details. Were you born and raised in New York?"

"Would you really like to know?"

"Only if you want to tell me. If it's a secret…"

"Not a big deal." He said the words casually, but she sensed that remembering bothered him. She should have kept her curiosity to herself and let him volunteer the information if he wanted to share.

Creed tapped his fork on his empty plate and then set it aside. "We were poor."

She glanced around the kitchen at the high-quality furniture and recalled how she had overheard that his brothers bought Marquette's on a whim. If they were poor in the real sense, they had come a long way.

Creed seemed to pick up on her doubt. "There were days we had no food in the house and no money to buy any." He tipped his chin toward the refrigerator. "A small token of that time for me. I never allow it to be empty, no matter how infrequently I'm home."

"Marisa could explain that."

He raised his eyebrows in question.

"She loves psychology and takes endless classes on it for no reason other than that she loves it. I've heard her say the kids who've had a tough childhood often grow up to have vices, but they're all different from one another. Like one might spend too much money. Another might hoard it."

"Interesting," he commented. "I suppose she's right. My brothers and I are different."

"But you're close too. I can see it in the way you all interact with one another. You look out for them."

He frowned. "They're stubborn as jackasses."

She wanted to say, "Look who's talking," but kept quiet.

He eyed her, amused, reading her thoughts, no doubt. "My dad was an entertainer. He played the guitar and sang in nightclubs."

"No way."

He nodded. "Didn't go far, since half the time he either didn't come home or, when he did, came home drunk, angry, and broke." His mouth tightened, and she noticed how his knuckles, white from the grip on his coffee cup, stood out. "Stefan wanted to be just like him, but he didn't see what a loser the guy was."

She tut-tutted. "When they're really young, kids seldom do see the fault in their parents."

"I stood between him and my brothers when he came looking for a fight."

She gasped and touched his hand. "Creed, you aren't

that much older than them, are you? You shouldn't have had to do that."

He shrugged. "I'm thirty-five. Damen is thirty-three, and Stefan is thirty. You see the smile Stefan always has on his face. I did what I needed to in order to keep it there."

Anger radiated off him, and she guessed if he had something to pound at that moment—maybe even his dad—he would have used it. Then he smiled, and she felt like the sun shined.

"What's so funny?" she asked, glad his mood had lightened.

"Stefan. One day my mom was out at a job interview. We'd eaten up everything we had in the house, and I got a bone-headed idea of how to take care of it."

She took in his form. Creed must be at least six foot three or four. What had he looked like as a kid or as a teenager? Regardless, if he ate then the way he ate now, it was no wonder they had no food. Especially with their father's neglect.

"What did you do?" she asked.

"Well, I was going to steal."

Shada gasped. "Oh no. Tell me you weren't caught."

He grinned. "No, but do you know the bakery on Ninth?"

"Yes! I've been there. Love their chocolate rolls. Mmm."

"Don't make that noise."

She grinned at the arrested look on his face. "Go on."

"As I said, I intended to steal, and I chose that bakery. I told Stefan to stay home, and I took Damen with me. Unbeknown to Damen and me, Stefan had his own ideas of how to raise money. Damen and I were all set to distract the woman at the counter when we heard someone that sounded suspiciously like Stefan singing at the top of his lungs while he played guitar."

Shada burst out laughing. "Oh wow, don't tell me he did it right outside."

"Right outside the window. We could look through and see him standing there."

"Aw, that's so cute."

Creed growled. "I considered cracking his skull, except by the time Damen and I ran out of the store, he'd collected five dollars."

"No way."

"Way." Creed ran fingers through his hair, making it worse. She itched to touch it herself, but she knew what his hair felt like to touch. Much of the night, she had enjoyed tugging at it. In fact, it was probably her fault that it looked such a mess.

Shaking herself, she tried to focus on what Creed was saying. "So I'm guessing the rest was history?"

"Not exactly history. We were run off from the bakery. The owner didn't appreciate us blocking the entrance, but the three of us agreed singing might be a safer way to get money."

She gaped at him, surprised and impressed. "You sang?"

His cheeks reddened, and he grumbled in annoyance. "I might have helped a little."

"I'd like to hear you sing some time."

"Don't hold your breath." He stood up. "Come on. I need to get you home."

"I have to wash the dishes."

"I'll take care of it."

"Creed."

"You cooked. I wash. *Later*. It's a tradeoff."

From the stubborn set of his shoulders, she figured she couldn't change his mind, so she gave in. Besides, she wanted to go home and check on Marisa.

Creed dropped her off, and she let herself into the tiny apartment she shared with her sister. They had decorated it with the treasures they'd found over the years in New York's thrift stores. From brass giraffes to unsigned landscapes, she loved it all because it reflected their style. Yet, after being in Creed's house, she had to wonder what he would think of her home.

Who cares? It was just sex. Remember that.

As she passed through the living room, Shada noticed that the pile of four-inch thick books Marisa had been reading at the dining-room table the day before were now on the floor next to the coffee table. She frowned. How many times had she told Marisa to wait for her to move the books?

Shada reached her sister's room, knocked once, and opened the door. She smiled on seeing Marisa's tangled red hair fanning her pillow. A small fist had been tucked beneath her chin, and Marisa's long lashes brushed her cheeks. Shada inched on tiptoe over to the bed, stepping around more books as she went. Her heart constricted as she peered down at Marisa. Her sister might be twenty-eight, but in sleep, she looked no older than twelve. Shada sighed, and Marisa blinked up at her.

"Morning," Marisa whispered.

"I'm sorry. I didn't mean to wake you."

"I was getting up."

Shada sank down on the side of the bed. "I thought I told you to wait and let me move your books. I don't want you to wear yourself out. Don't be so stubborn."

Marisa looked away. "I...uh..."

Shada waited. "You uh what?" She leaned forward and squinted at her sister. Nobody knew Marisa like she did. They had come through a lot together, and the one thing Shada was sure of was that Marisa had a hard time lying to her. When Shada caught her doing things she shouldn't, like lifting heavy books, Marisa owned up to it and apologized. This was different, and Shada didn't like it. She reached out to touch Marisa's chin, but she didn't force her sister to look her in the eyes. "Spill it, you."

Marisa gave a weak grin. "I didn't exactly move them."

"Come again?"

Her sister shifted under the covers, and Shada stood to let her rise. As usual, Marisa took a good minute to sit up, and she sat in silence on the side of the bed. She rubbed her eyes and hauled thick, unruly hair out of her face. Shada looked on with affection and impatience. She had been looking after Marisa almost from the day they met in foster care, when Marisa's parents abandoned the sickly little eight-year-old.

Thinking about the past, Shada almost forgot what she had asked.

Marisa spoke, pulling her from unhappy memories. "Damen moved them for me."

"He did what?" Shada's voice rose. "What the hell was Damen doing in our apartment? Why was he here when I wasn't home?"

Marisa almost never grew angry with Shada, although Shada flew off the handle all the time. Not necessarily with Marisa, but just at life and circumstances in general. Marisa tended to dig her heels in until Shada coaxed her to listen to reason. Now she firmed her deep rose lips in a way that warned Shada what was coming.

"I'm not a child, Shada. Don't talk to me like one."

"Oh, excuse me." Shada folded her arms across her chest. "You sure are acting like one."

"How? I had a man over."

"Yes, a womanizer."

"You don't know that."

"And you don't know men, Marisa. I don't want you hurt. Anyone can see he's not serious from a mile away."

"Creed was last night?"

Shada's teeth clicked when she snapped them together. She sighed and ran a hand over Marisa's hair. Good thing she didn't need to come in early, because she saw them spending a couple hours getting her sister's hair untangled and washed.

"I understand what Creed wants, and he understands me. No, it's not serious. You know I don't want to get involved with anyone."

Marisa hugged her, and Shada watched the fire in her eyes die out, as it always did, to be replaced by sweet happiness. "You say that, but deep inside you want to be loved, and you want to love."

Shada groaned. "Don't go there. Besides, this isn't about me. We're talking about you."

"I'm fine."

"Marisa."

"At some point, you're going to have to stop worrying about me."

"No, I don't."

Marisa chuckled and then coughed. Shada rubbed her back and then pulled a lock of hair from Marisa's mouth. She started at the warm skin and felt Marisa's forehead.

"You feel hot."

"I'm okay."

"You're not." Shada hurried to the dresser to get the kit containing various items she needed for Marisa. She found the thermometer and stuck it in her sister's ear. A second later, the unit beeped, and Shada read it. "One hundred degrees. What time did you go to bed?"

"Not too late."

"Sis." This time Shada did make Marisa meet her gaze. "What time?"

"Um…one, maybe?"

Shada swore. "Because he kept you up! I don't want you to see him anymore, Marisa."

Her sister said nothing.

"Marisa, when you don't get enough rest, you get sick. You know that."

"I'm okay."

"Damn it, you're so stubborn, and I have to nurse you after you do something like this."

Shada realized her mistake the second the words left her lips. She really didn't mean it. She was just pissed that Marisa wouldn't listen, and that damned Damen probably only thought of his cock.

"You don't have to take care of me." Marisa lay down again and burrowed beneath the covers. "I can take care of myself."

"Sis, I'm sorry. I didn't mean it." Shada reached for her, but Marisa shook her hand off.

"I said I'm fine," came the muffled response.

"I love you," Shada tried.

Nothing.

Shada headed to the door. She went to the kitchen and prepared Marisa breakfast, tea, and her morning meds. Then she brought everything back on a tray. After setting the tray on the table next to Marisa's bed, she sat down and waited. Marisa rolled over and sat up. Slowly, she began to eat. Shada's heart ached as she watched the labored movements. No matter what, Marisa said she was fine, but there were days like today when she had no energy, when her temperature rose, and she needed more time in bed. What got them both through were the better days. Rested and somehow stronger, Marisa would attend psych classes, eat lunch out with Shada, and even do a limited amount of shopping. Shada lived for those days and would spend as much time as possible with her sister to enjoy them.

When Marisa finished eating, Shada watched over her while she took her medicine and then gathered the dishes. At Marisa's bedroom door, her sister called out to her.

Shada balanced the tray on one hip and glanced over her shoulder. "Yes?"

Marisa lay in bed with the covers pulled to her chin. "I love you too."

Shada blew her a kiss and left the room, sniffling. She

spent the rest of the morning caring for her sister and then left her sleeping to head in to work. Shada's anger hadn't cooled by the time she reached Marquette's. In fact, the closer she drew to the place, the higher her own temperature rose. If Damen thought he was getting his jollies off with Marisa, he had another think coming. She would beat him with a frying pan in his own restaurant if she had to.

When Shada strode through the door at work, she didn't have to search for Damen. He stood in the main dining room, leaning against a column and smiling down at Tiffany. So much tinier than the tall, lanky man, she tilted her head way back, exposing her throat as if she offered it to him. Tiffany said something, and Damen chuckled. She reached up to touch his glasses and ran a finger along the frame.

Shada clenched her hands at her sides and weaved through the tables. "Enjoying youself?" she demanded of Damen.

His eyebrows went up. "I try to get enjoyment out of each day."

She rolled her eyes. "I bet. I need to talk to you—*alone*. If you can pry yourself away from Ms. Thing for a minute."

Tiffany pouted and laid a hand on Damen's chest. "Really, Shada, you come barging in here all angry, as usual. I was talking to Damen. Surely, whatever you want can wait."

Shada narrowed her eyes and she raised a finger as she stepped toward the woman. "Let me tell you something, bitch—"

"Whoa, it's fine." Damen thrust Tiffany to the side before Shada could get to her. He gestured toward the back. "How about we talk in the office, Shada. Creed had an errand and will be back soon."

Shada capitulated, but she caught Tiffany's complaint behind her. "Why does everyone always give in to her? She's not that scary."

"I think you better shut up, Tiff," another of the waitresses said, and Shada ignored them both to follow Damen into the kitchen and farther back to the office.

As soon as the door shut, she rounded on him. "Stay the hell away from my sister."

His eyebrows rose. "Don't you think that's up to her?"

"No. I've been looking after her since I was thirteen, and I've sent sneakier men than you about their business."

"Sneaky?" She had offended him, judging by the tone of his voice, but she didn't care. Damen frowned. "Marisa and I are friends. There's nothing wrong with it. She's an adult. Besides, we both enjoy psychology."

"Come off it. You just want to get in her panties. I know you were at my place last night, and then I find you up in Tiffany's face."

"We were talking, nothing more."

She glared at him. "Who? You and Marisa or you and Tiffany?"

"Both."

She moved closer to him. "Don't come to my house again. Ever."

"I think you need to show your boss a little bit more respect."

Now she saw his anger. She hadn't witnessed it before, but she refused to back down just because of who he was. "Me working for you has nothing to do with you trying to seduce my sister. You think because you give me a paycheck, I'm supposed to hand her over?"

Color stained his cheeks. "Of course not. I didn't mean it that way."

"How did you mean it, Damen?"

He grunted. "I don't mean her any harm, Shada. I'm a good guy. Ask anybody. Marisa is smart. I couldn't take advantage of her if I tried."

"And pretty."

He worked his jaw. "Fine, yes, she's very pretty. I wouldn't be a man if I didn't see that, but if I fuck her—"

Shada screamed. She leaped at Damen, her fingers curled like claws. He retreated a step, and she would have jumped after him if a strong arm didn't wrap itself around her waist from behind and haul her backward. She kicked at the legs of the man holding her, but he didn't flinch. His steel embrace meant she could scarcely draw in a breath, let alone escape.

"Out!" Creed ordered, his voice booming from somewhere above her head.

"Creed, just let me explain to her," Damen began.

"Now, Damen."

His brother left, and Shada shrieked after him. "Don't let him go! I'm going to beat him until he never goes near Marisa again."

The door shut behind Damen's retreating back.

"Coward," she shouted after him.

Creed hauled her across the room and dumped her into the chair behind his desk. She tried to rise, but he pressed a heavy hand on her shoulder to keep her where she sat. She scowled at him, but he had the nerve to plant his feet, and his huge frame blocked her from going after his brother.

"You *would* take his side."

"I'm not taking anyone's side, Shada."

She rolled her eyes and looked away.

"I returned and heard you shouting from the hall."

"I wasn't yelling until you grabbed me."

"Trust me, I heard you through the door, and probably everyone else did too. I'm glad we weren't in the middle of serving guests."

"That's all you care about." He pinned her with his steady, and surprisingly calm, gaze, and she sighed. "Look, I'm pissed, okay? I found out while we were … um …together, your brother was at my house."

"So?"

"So!"

"Shada, I'm not your enemy. Neither is Damen."

"That's what you say."

"Don't you think she has a right to see who she wants, Shada? Or have you been controlling her all her life?"

"I don't control Marisa." Guilt assailed her. "I love her. She's not strong. I worry."

"Of course."

Tears pricked her eyes. "She had a fever this morning, Creed. He kept her up too late. When that happens, she gets sick. Neither of you understand. She's all I've got."

He softened and leaned back on the desk in front of

her. When he held out his hand, she hesitated. He whispered her name, and she stood to lean on his chest. His arms came up around her, gentler this time, and she shut her eyes.

"I'll talk to him," he said.

"He was so coarse, talking about fucking her."

"Damen isn't a bad guy."

"He said that."

He chuckled. "He isn't. He can be stupid, I'll give you that, but he means no harm. Tell you what. I'll make it crystal clear that Marisa's to be treated with kid gloves. If he doesn't get it, I'll gladly bust his head for you."

"Naw, pal, you're not taking my satisfaction."

He laughed again. "You're hardcore."

She leaned away from him. "So you're not going to fire me for threatening to beat your brother's ass?"

His eyes crinkled at the edges. "Shada, if you were gone, where would I get my daily entertainment? You keep this place alive."

"Whatever. I'm going to work." She started to walk away, but he grabbed her hand to hold her back. "Let me go, Creed. I have work to do."

"Promise me you won't fight Damen in the restaurant."

She snatched her hand away and put it on her hip. "I can't make that promise."

"Shada."

"Fine. I won't fight him in the restaurant."

He glared at her. When he started to speak again, she muttered an excuse and hurried out of the office. Let him think he had solved everything, but she didn't like Damen, and it probably wasn't over between them. No matter what anyone said, she would defend Marisa. Even if she had to do it all alone and stand against a Marquette.

CHAPTER EIGHT

Two weeks had passed since Shada had slept with Creed. She hadn't seen him much, because he'd had to return to New York for his other business. Neither of them had mentioned getting together again, but Shada found she couldn't get him out of her head. He didn't make it any better when he texted her from where he was.

Describe to me what you're cooking, he wrote.

Why does that sound dirty? she replied.

Because you have a dirty mind.

You're crazy.

Come on, Shada. Tell me. I want to visualize it. I'm hungry.

She laughed as she read his words. *You're insane.*

She did go into detail, though, telling him all about the blackened stuffed pork tenderloin with celery, red bell peppers, shallots, onions, along with some chipotle, so it would be nice and spicy. When that got him excited, she included a description of how tender her cuts of meat were, so soft they would melt in his mouth. She reported on the dirty rice she had experimented with making and all the spices she had chosen for the dish. A few natives of New Orleans hadn't believed the chef didn't come from their fine state, and Shada proudly let Creed know this too. He praised her, warming her from her toes to the roots of her hair, and she had to rein in her emotions before she went too far.

Her strong attraction to Creed aside, Shada had to deal with both Marisa and Damen ignoring her warnings. Unfortunately, it also meant she got into more arguments with her sister, which she hated. The situation got to the point where she didn't want Marisa coming to work with her. Yet she couldn't deny Marisa's requests, because she liked to keep an eye on her, and they couldn't afford a full-time nurse. Not that Marisa needed one, as she often pointed out.

One particular Sunday afternoon, Shada glanced through the kitchen window and spotted Damen serving Marisa a glass of sweet tea. He lingered at her elbow, listening while she spoke to him. Shada frowned and started out the door, but Tiffany bound through it, almost knocking her down.

Shada paused at the sight of the full plate of food in Tiffany's hand. "What's that?" she asked.

Tiffany smirked. "What does it look like? The customer at table nine says the sauce isn't fresh, and it doesn't taste the way it did the last time she was here."

"What?" Shada snatched the plate. "I made that not even an hour ago."

"Maybe you missed a step," the skank said, and Shada worked on quelling the impulse to dump the food on her head.

"What's wrong?"

Creed appeared, and somehow her body came alive. He'd been back all of two days, and she couldn't stop staring when he walked into the room. Neither of them had approached the other on a personal basis, and the texts he had teased her with stopped when he returned. Now she began to think he must have been in boring meetings and had been looking for a way to distract himself. Silly her, she should have realized.

"Oh, Creed," Tiffany simpered. She touched his arm. "The customer at table nine isn't happy with the sauce, and Shada won't take responsibility for skimping."

Creed's eyes flashed annoyance. "Shada doesn't skimp when it comes to cooking."

Shada snapped her fingers in Tiffany's face, and the woman looked fit to catch fire where she stood. She flipped her ponytail and pursed her lips.

Creed peered through the window and nodded. "Got it. Rene, another plate, please. Shada, the sauce."

She frowned. "But the customer didn't like it."

He smiled. "Trust me."

"I do."

The words slipped out, but Creed didn't appear to notice. He whipped out of the kitchen, with Tiffany tripping after him. Shada watched through the window as Creed bent over the woman in a semi-bow and offered her the fresh food with a flourish. One would have thought from the grace of his movement that he hailed from the eighteen hundreds, yet his size also reminded her of a jungle cat—sexy but dangerous.

Shada couldn't hear what the woman said, but she gushed with obvious pleasure. A hand invariably went to her bosom, with the other brushing Creed's arm. Shada tried not to gag as she spun away. She returned to her work, rushing about but taking great care at each step to make food Marquette's would be proud to serve.

Creed entered the kitchen moments later. "Fire extinguished."

She made a rude noise. "Of course, she did it to get your attention or that of one of your brothers."

He shrugged. "A part of the game."

"Does the game include Damen lingering at Marisa's table?"

He moved too close to her. Her heart raced, and she found it hard to draw in a steady breath. When he reached out, she thought he was about to touch her—in front of the kitchen staff—but he flicked a finger against the pot where she had made the sauce. "I was called away to New York, but I'm back now. I'll talk to him tonight as I promised. And don't worry. I know personally how good your sauce is."

Shada blinked after him as he disappeared into his office. Unless her mind had fallen permanently into the gutter, he had just made a sexual innuendo. *No, I'm reading something into it. I just got a complaint, and he must have thought I was worried about continuing my specialties.*

The self-talk did nothing to calm her down, and she reminded herself while she worked that it was a good thing

Creed had backed off and didn't ask to take her home again. She needed cool-down time, a minute to get things straight in her head. They had fun together. Nothing wrong with that, but that was all it was. All it could be.

The rest of the day passed quickly, with Shada moving nonstop. New guests arrived as fast as the previous ones left, and the next time she looked up, it was pushing six in the evening. She gasped, realizing she had forgotten about seeing Marisa home. Flying to the front dining room, she called out to Rene. "Be right back. I have to see to my sister."

He said something she didn't hear, and the door closed behind her. A couple occupied the table where Marisa had sat earlier. Shada scanned the restaurant and didn't spot her sister, so she checked the private rooms on the second floor. All were empty, so she walked back to the kitchen while digging in her pocket for her cell phone. Halfway down the hall toward Creed's office, she dialed Marisa's number, but there was no answer. Worry stirred in her heart. When Creed called "Come" to her knock, she barreled in.

He stood when he saw the look on her face. "What's wrong, Shada?"

"Marisa isn't answering her phone, and I don't know where she is."

His expression changed.

"You know something about this, don't you?"

He held up his hands as he approached her. "I talked to Damen."

"And?"

"And he promised to look after her."

Shada went cold. "Look after her *when?*"

"Don't freak out, baby."

She flinched at his calling her baby, since he hadn't acted like they still had anything going on. When he saw her reaction, he corrected himself and called her by name. She didn't know which was worse.

"Shada, they're friends. He took her to dinner."

"They could have eaten together here."

He raised his brows.

"I know I'm being stupid, but…"

"I get it. You're worried. It's just dinner. I'm sure she knows how you feel, and she'll call."

As soon as he said it, her cell phone rang, and she blew out a breath in relief at the sight of Marisa's name. Shada stabbed the connect button. "Marisa, are you okay?"

Her sister laughed. "I'm fine. Sorry I didn't answer." She lowered her voice and whispered into the phone, "I had to…"

All kinds of terrible thoughts popped into Shada's head.

"… I had to pee."

Shada laughed. "You're nuts. Are you sure you're fine?"

"Yes, we're just getting our food. You know I'm with Damen, don't you?"

"You didn't let me know you were going."

"You were busy."

"I'm sorry, sis."

"It's okay, Shada. You're working. I don't expect you to babysit me. Damen and I are going to have some fun."

"Please, sis, don't overdo it."

"I won't, Mom. We'll even be back by eight-thirty, just in time for bed."

"Haha, very funny. I'll talk to you later, and you can tell me all about your date."

"You got it. Good night."

"Night," Shada echoed, and she disconnected the call. Worry clogged her mind, no matter how many times she told herself to chill. Creed laid a hand at her waist, but she moved out of reach. "I have to get back out there. Thanks."

"Shada."

She kept moving, pretending she didn't hear him.

———

Shada squeezed off a ball of strawberry sherbet into a dessert dish and balanced a macaroon cookie, made with white chocolate Satsuma ganache, in the center. The decadent treat had been a hit, and Creed had spoken of opening a gift shop in one of the unused areas of the restaurant to offer the macaroons and other goodies. She felt like he was bringing to life ideas she had never even dreamed of, let alone hoped would one day come true.

In truth, Rene's creations always got more fanfare than hers from their guests, but she didn't mind. She had lots to learn and was enjoying the ride.

"Non! Not like that."

She looked up from her task. Think of the devil, and there he appeared. Rene's expression was that of a man who had just seen a train wreck. Dramatic. He waved spindly arms and rushed over to her. She loved his Cajun accent, but it was too bad his pock-marked skin kept him from being attractive. Maybe he was to someone.

She straightened and studied the dessert. "What's wrong with it?"

"Where's the syrup?" he demanded. Rene snapped his fingers, and another of the kitchen staff zipped over with the strawberry syrup. With a flourish, Rene dressed up her treat, making it that much more beautiful. She should have thought of such a simple addition. Rene nodded his approval. "Perfect."

She smiled. "Thanks."

"Quickly," Rene barked, and the assistant whisked the dish away, ready to hand it off to Tiffany or one of the other servers.

With everyone moving at high speed and more and more diners arriving all the time, Shada didn't have more than a moment here and there to think about her sister. However, her pace came to a screeching halt when Creed blew into the kitchen, took her arm, and propelled her toward the door.

"Come with me," he said without explanation, hurrying her along. He called over his shoulder. "Get someone to cover for her, Rene. She won't be back tonight."

Shada stumbled to keep up with him. "What's this about, Creed? Would you slow the hell down?"

They reached the back alley, and she gaped when a car pulled up and a man jumped out and handed the keys to Creed. Creed ushered her into the passenger seat and then took the wheel. Soon, they were out of the alley and on Royal Street, headed toward Conti.

"I want you to stay calm, Shada," he said. "Do you think you can do that?"

Her stomach turned. "Why would I need to stay calm?"

He hesitated and glanced at her. When he reached for her hand, she let him take it, but only because she suspected she might need it. "Marisa collapsed. She's okay, but Damen took her to the hospital just in case."

Shada's world dipped and swayed. She squeezed Creed's hand and pressed her lips together, saying nothing.

"You okay?" he asked.

She didn't respond. After an eternity, they drew up to the hospital, and she jumped out of the car even as Creed pressed the brakes. Let him find parking on his own. She ran to the emergency entrance and burst through the sliding doors to get to the information desk. "Marisa Cobalt, where is she?"

The woman behind the counter smiled. "Are you family?"

"I'm her sister. I need to get back there."

Maybe she had Marisa's stats on her computer, but the woman frowned in confusion. She opened her mouth to speak, but Shada cut her off.

"I know, I know. I'm black, she's white. Ever heard of adoption? I'm all the family she's got. Let me back where she is. Now!"

What Shada said wasn't really true. Marisa still had family, and they had never adopted Shada. Her fear, and maybe the fact that she was on the verge of tears, convinced the woman, and she buzzed Shada through the doors and directed her on where to go. Just as she hurried to them, Creed arrived and followed.

They found Marisa lying pale and still on a bed, and Shada darted to her side. At first, she didn't even see Damen until he spoke.

"I'm sorry, Shada. I would have called sooner, but I didn't know your number, and I had rushed Marisa here and left her phone in the car. I called my brother to get you."

Shada rounded on him. "What the hell were you doing?"

His gaze shifted to Creed, who hadn't spoken. "I …uh…we went bowling."

Shada didn't think before she acted. One minute she stood beside the bed, holding Marisa's hand. The next she cracked Damen in the jaw, and she almost fell on the floor at the pain.

"Shada!" Creed grabbed her and dragged her into his arms.

Damen didn't so much as stumble backward. His head snapped away a couple of inches, and he raised a hand to his mouth, eyes wide with shock.

Shada cradled her hand in her lap while trying to get out of Creed's arms.

"Damn it, stay still and let me look at your hand," he growled.

"I don't need your help." She tried to jerk away, but he wouldn't be put off. He grabbed her wrist, making the pain worse.

"Move your fingers," he commanded.

"Back off, Creed. I need to have a conversation with your brother."

"You've said everything with your fists, and you might have broken your hand."

"Please, I didn't hit him that hard."

"Shada?" came a soft call, and they both froze. Marisa had awakened, and Shada wiggled away from

106

Creed to get to her bedside. She brushed her sister's hair from her face. "Sis, what happened? Are you okay?"

Marisa gave a sheepish smile. "I think I overdid it."

"Really?" Shada bit off the sarcasm the best she could. "It's not *your* fault."

Before Marisa could defend the bastard she'd gone out with, a doctor walked into the room. "Well, look what we have here, a family of loved ones. That's always nice, but we have a two visitor limit, and Ms. Cobalt needs to rest."

Shada stared at Damen. "Is she going to be okay, doctor?"

"I believe so, with rest," he assured her. "We've been informed of her condition, and the best Ms. Cobalt can do at this time is take her prescribed medicines, get plenty of rest, and follow-up with her GP." He waggled a finger at Marisa. "I'm sure after so long, you're familiar with how far to take your activities. Just take it easy, and you'll be fine."

Shada sighed in relief. "Will she stay the night?"

"She can be moved to a room for the night, but it isn't necessary. Whatever you prefer. Just make sure she rests at home, at least a few days of very light activity."

The doctor left with the intention of ordering release papers since Marisa insisted on going home.

Shada gave Creed a pointed look, and he dragged his brother from the room. Shada sat down beside her sister and kissed her cheek.

"What were you thinking?" Shada asked.

Marisa smiled, unrepentant. She seemed so much frailer than usual, but it could have been a figment of Shada's imagination. Marisa was pale, with little color even in her usually rosy lips. "I had so much fun with Damen."

"He had you bowling!"

"I didn't lift any balls."

"Well, what was the point, then?"

Marisa shrugged. "Just watching him do it for the both of us. He sucks. Bad."

Despite herself, Shada chuckled, but her fear returned. She bundled Marisa up and let Creed take them both home. When Damen tried to speak to her at their apartment door, she slammed it in his face.

Marisa didn't complain. In fact, she stayed silent, and Shada knew she was beat. Shada put her to bed with the intention of helping her to shower the next morning. All night, she sat at Marisa's bedside and watched her in between nodding off herself. Over the next few days, she took off from work to care for her.

CHAPTER NINE

Shada slammed a pot on the stove and then forgot what the heck she intended to do with it. She stomped to the larder and wrenched the door open, as if that would hurt anyone. The vast store of food lay before her, but for the first time, nothing appealed. She went in anyway and grabbed random items. Putting them on the counter, she added eggs, peppers, and steak. She cracked the eggs into a bowl and crumbled half the shells in as well.

"Damn it!" she screamed and threw the bowl into the sink. Good thing the bowl is made of stainless steel, she thought after the fact. Another try produced the same effect, and the clank of metal to metal did nothing to calm her rage.

"Hey!"

Shada scowled at Creed, not having realized he was there. She had hoped, with it being so late, no one would be around, and she could work out her frustrations alone. "Why are you here?" she demanded.

He strode over to her and removed the tenth egg from her fingers. "I work here, remember? What's wrong?"

"Nothing. Just leave me alone."

"I can't do that." He stepped closer. Her desire stirred, but it pissed her off, and she retreated. He followed and kissed her lips. A moan hovered in her throat, but she swallowed it. Somehow she managed to resist and turned her head. When she raised a hand to smack his face, he caught her wrist. She tried with the other hand, and he caught that one to jerk her against him. "You've done enough."

"What's that's supposed to mean?" She pulled on his hold. "Let me go, Creed."

"Not until you calm down."

"Fuck you."

He released her wrists and grabbed her shoulders to shake her. She fought as hard as she could, thrusting at his chest, beating against it like some lame little damsel from a romance. The more she did—and failed—the more her temper soared. Only exhaustion made her stop fighting him, and she panted, arms aching at her side.

"Better?" he said, backing up.

She said nothing.

He touched her hair, and she spun away to look at the royal mess she had made of the kitchen. Still, she made no move to clean it up just yet. Her emotions were too raw.

"She's fine, Shada," he said. "You told me so yourself this morning."

"I know."

"She's been sleeping most of the time for a few days now, and you told me today was the first time she seemed back to normal."

"Normal." Her laugh sounded more like a sob. "Everything you're saying is true. Her doctor even said she's okay, well, as much as can be expected."

"Then you need to unwind."

"I'm fine."

"No, you're not."

She cut her eyes over at him. "Are you telling me I need a drink?"

He didn't answer but turned and headed down the hall to his office. She followed, and he let her in and shut the door behind them.

"Creed?"

"I don't drink."

"You don't?" She frowned, trying to recall if during any of the times they had all celebrated together she had seen him with a glass of wine. She couldn't remember. "Because of your dad?"

He shrugged. "Come here, Shada."

"Your brothers both drink."

He stood near his desk and held out his hand. "Now."

She wandered over to him, and he took her hand and whipped her around until she stumbled. He smacked her ass hard, and she cried out, loving it. The dress she had worn was thrust up to her waist, and he shredded her panties just as he had done before. She stared at them as they fluttered in pieces to the floor. Creed smacked her now-bare ass again, and the sting brought tears to her eyes. He stroked her skin there and squeezed. She leaned on the desk for support.

He dropped to his knees behind her and kissed one cheek. "If you want to calm down, I'll help you," he said.

Calm down? He drove her to the brink of an orgasm with a few kisses and a spanking. How was that calming her? Yet his actions had eased a little of the frustration. If they continued, she might find release—emotionally and physically.

"Now you ask me?" she teased. "After you've destroyed my panties? I need to bill you for all my clothes."

"I'll give you whatever you want."

She bit her lip. He was serious, the way he looked up at her. She might have been higher than him at that moment, but she sensed his strength and control. Even from that position, he held all the cards.

Shada forced her gaze from his and peered at the window. Heavy curtains kept anyone who might be passing in the alley from seeing in. Out in the restaurant, all lay in silence, now that she'd stopped slamming pots and pans.

"I'm not looking to be any man's mistress."

Creed bumped the insides of her legs, and she spread them wider. He ran a hand over her dripping pussy, up past it to her belly, and down again to cup her mound. A pulse started in her core. She swallowed.

"You already belong to me, and we both know it."

She turned to face him and started to walk away. He

stood and caught her around the waist, spun her to face the desk, and cornered her with his large frame. A hand on either side of her hips trapped her even more, and she licked her lips. Her heart raced, and the blood pulsing in her ears made it hard to hear.

Creed reached around and raised her chin with one finger. He kissed her lips, parted them with the tip of his tongue, and dipped inside for an instant. When he drew away, she almost whined in disappointment.

Creed tapped a finger on her mouth. "These lips are mine." He grazed her pussy with two fingers. "This pussy is mine." He placed a hand across the front of her hips to protect her from the desk and smacked her ass. She bumped against his arm, whimpered, and grabbed onto him for support. "This ass is mine."

She said nothing. Emotion bubbled up inside, and her pussy clenched so much with need she couldn't find words to speak.

"Now, you can say our word, but you damn sure better say it fast, Shada. Because when I open my pants, I'm going to put my dick in you."

"R-right here?" She never thought he could take her to greater heights than he had the night they'd had sex for the first time.

He threaded his fingers into her pussy and stroked in and out. She was so wet, her juices coated his digits, and she moaned, arching her back and pressing her ass into his crotch.

"Do you want to tell me no, baby?"

How could anyone tell him no? "I…no…"

He pushed his fingers inside her and left them there, his palm flat on her mound. "No is not our word, Shada. What's our word?"

She forgot.

"Shada?" The crackle of a condom packet sounded in the room. She felt his movements as he raised a hand to tear it open with his teeth. Her pussy pulsed around his fingers, but he didn't move them. He kept them buried deep inside her, and she couldn't help thinking about what she would feel next. His cock, all thick and hard, would soon replace his hand. She wanted it bad. She wanted him to spank her some more and, when he fucked her, to pump until her pussy ached.

Dragon. The word popped into her head. She bit her tongue, refusing to utter the word. Creed's hand abandoned her, and she could have wept. "No," she whispered.

The condom snapped into place, and he held her hip with one hand. The other, he used to guide the tip of his shaft to her opening. Shada went up onto her toes and arched until her ass cheeks spread. Creed pierced her moist entrance and groaned. He slid in an inch at a time, driving her crazy.

"All of it," she begged. "Give it to me, Creed."

"You'll get it when I say, not before."

She pushed back on him, but he pressed her forward, pinning her against the desk. He thrust aside papers and pens, and the rest of the items on his desk tumbled to the floor. With a large hand in the center of her back, he forced her to lie on the wooden surface. Her breasts flattened and her nipples tight, she shut her eyes and waited.

Creed rewarded her for rushing him with a spanking. She curled her fingers around the edge of the desk as an orgasm began to build. The *thwack* of his palm meeting her flesh sent desire higher.

"Creed," she whispered.

He massaged her ass cheeks and pulled them wide. Gently, his cock wove between her folds, and he sank deep into her pussy. She shook from head to toe. With her ass still stinging from the spanking, Creed began pumping into her. He moved slow and easy at first, but almost right away, he picked up the pace. Her lover knew what they both enjoyed.

"Do you want it faster, baby?" he asked.

"Yes!"

"Do you need my cock?"

"Yes, please," she begged.

"Raise your knee."

She placed a hand at her side to brace herself and then raised one knee onto the desk. Creed thrust harder. She screamed in delight. He pounded deeper. Her core muscles contracted, driving her higher and higher. Surely, she couldn't get any wetter than she already was, and yet her body felt as if it would combust any second. Creed leaned over her and reached with one hand to the opposite side of the desk. He used the leverage to pound harder. She cried out his name. Their bodies slapped together again and again, the noises they made adding to the pleasure. Ecstasy took her mind and made it impossible to think. All she could do was feel him, love how he ravaged her pussy and claimed it as his own.

"Play with your clit," he ordered and pulled her back a little so she could reach the bud. While he kept up his rhythm, Shada pinched her clit between her thumb and forefinger. She gave it a tug and rubbed over the surface. An orgasm roared through her body. She called out to him. He didn't slow down but encouraged her to do it again. In between small pauses, during which she was too sensitive to touch, she brought herself to orgasm several times. At last, Creed thrust into her and held himself in to the hilt. He muttered something, and then she felt the pulse. He had come.

After a moment to catch his breath, Creed pulled out. He helped her to rise and drew her into his arms, facing him. Shada welcomed his tongue into her mouth and his strong embrace. "You're calmer now, aren't you?"

"I might be," she joked.

He brushed a hand over her thigh, and she wondered what condition her dress lay in. The last time he had ruined her clothes, she'd gone home in some oversized ones of his. She'd taken her only change of clothes home to wash and had forgotten to bring them back today.

"Who's here?" came a booming voice down the hall.

Shada and Creed froze. Fear tightened her belly. For some reason, Rene had showed up at the restaurant. Oh hell, she didn't want him to see her in the state she was in, and there wasn't a doubt in her mind the office smelled like sex.

Creed held up a finger to her lips and then darted to the door. He locked it and shut off the lights. The office was plunged into total darkness.

"Creed?" she whispered.

"Open the curtains, Shada," came the low reply.

She managed to get around the desk and pull back the curtain. Moonlight illuminated the office enough for her to see him standing near the door. He gestured for her to come to him, and she hurried over. As soon as she reached him, Creed tugged her to his chest and kissed her lips. A sound outside the door made them freeze again. She started to speak, but Creed covered her mouth. Her heart hammered so loud, it was a wonder Rene didn't hear it through the door.

Rene moved away, but she heard him fussing in French. She didn't understand a word, but he must be pissed at the mess in the kitchen. "I'm going out there. I don't want him to think I left it that way."

Creed pulled her hand off the doorknob. "You can explain it to him later, when I'm finished with you."

She grinned in the darkness, scarcely able to see his face but sure his eyes glittered with lust. Nothing could dampen it, including the risk of discovery. Meanwhile, she felt like she might collapse with nerves.

"We can't do it again, with Rene so close."

Another condom appeared from nowhere, it seemed. She started to pull away. He caught her. Creed put her silently against the door, legs spread, the head of his cock against her pussy. The man was already hard again.

Or maybe he never went soft.

"Are you telling me no?"

Damn him. She moaned. "Creed, you know I can't tell you no."

He sank inside her. She started to cry out, but he covered her mouth. A wonderful pounding began again, and Shada decided to put off until tomorrow thinking about whether Rene could identify where the steady thump against the door had come from. All she cared about right now was pleasing her man and being pleasured by him the rest of the night.

In the light of day—well, four o' clock might not be the light of day, but it was technically another day—Shada questioned whether she'd lost her everlasting mind. She did her best to clean up in the bathroom off Creed's office, and then she tossed her panties in a grocery bag before stuffing them under a pile of papers in his trashcan. Her pussy was sore, again, and Creed had left her alone to go speak with Rene, who had never left the restaurant. How the heck was she going to show her face out there? This was crazy. Her obsession with Creed had to have some boundaries, some freaking rules.

When she forced herself to go to the kitchen, her muttered, "Morning," to Rene was met with a grunted response. He didn't even turn around. She saw that the mess she had made was now gone, and she grimaced. "Um, sorry about the state of the kitchen. I meant to clean it up before anyone else arrived."

No comment.

"Well, I'm not due in until this afternoon, so I'm going home," she said. "I'll see you later."

"Bonjou."

She sighed and walked out to the main dining room. Before she reached the front door, Creed called to her, and she glanced back. He approached her, looking remarkably fresh for someone who hadn't slept all night. She was pretty sure she looked a hot mess.

"I want to talk to you," he said.

"Not now, Creed. I'm tired, and I probably stink."

He grinned. "You don't. You smell like—"

"Don't even. What did you want to talk about?"

"Us."

Butterflies stirred in her stomach. Did he expect her to get any sleep before her shift? "There's not really anything to talk about."

"There is. How about ten, my office?"

"Don't you have to prepare for the lunchtime rush?" She was so glad she had the time off today. The prep for dinner was all she was responsible for. Tomorrow, Rene was off, and she would be the one in charge. She looked forward to it.

"I'm adjusting my schedule to suit yours. Besides, all I do is put out an occasional fire."

She smirked. "Please, you know you're more valuable than that."

He touched her cheek with the back of his knuckles, and a shiver ran down her spine. "Thanks. So ten?"

"Fine, but not your office. A café or something."

He agreed to meet her at Marquette's and then for the two of them to walk over to the café on Royal. She left him then and headed home. First, she checked on Marisa and found her sister sleeping peacefully. Afterward, she showered and dropped naked into her own bed. Brushing her bare skin, the sheets were a reminder of how Creed's hands had felt doing the same thing. She shut her eyes, and images of their office adventure came flooding back. And then there was his insistence that they talk about them. There was no "us" as far as she knew, except he had called her body his earlier. Maybe he wasn't ready to stop having sex with her. She didn't blame him. They were good together, physically, and she'd be lying if she said she had had enough. If a woman could get enough of Creed's body, Shada knew nothing of it.

Rather than sleeping, she lay awake all morning, going over and over what she wanted if Creed said he wanted a standing arrangement between them. Could that be it? She'd said she was no man's mistress, because she didn't like the connotations of it. Yet in this day and age, it wasn't about the man alone, about meeting *his* needs. Hell, Creed could be *her* paramour. She laughed at the ridiculousness of it, especially since neither of them were married.

At nine, Shada climbed out of bed in defeat. She brushed her teeth, washed her face, and dressed. Marisa met her in the kitchen, and Shada kissed the top of her sister's head. "Hungry?"

"Not really, but since I know you'll lecture me on the importance of keeping my strength up, I'll have bacon and eggs, please."

Shada eyed her sister. "Someone wake up on the wrong side of the bed?"

Marisa groaned. "I'm sorry. I'm just…"

"What?" Shada sank down into a chair opposite Marisa and took her hands. "You don't usually get up without me waking you. Did you sleep badly?"

"Not exactly."

"Sis, you're starting to worry me."

Marisa groaned and pulled her hands from Shada's. "I'm in a foul mood because I feel like I have to tell you something."

"Spill it." Both Creed and Marisa wanted to rob her of peace. Why they had to offer cryptic hints about needing to talk, she didn't know, but she was over it already.

"I..." Marisa swallowed.

Shada did her best to wait in silence. Patience didn't enter into the equation.

Marisa rubbed her arms. She wore a heavy winter nightie, even though the temperature outside was warm, and beneath it, Shada guessed, her sister wore socks.

"I had sex," she blurted.

Shada blinked at her. Now that she could respond, she had nothing.

"You're not saying anything, Shada." Marisa twisted her hands. Why did she come off looking like a teenager confessing to her mother about being sexually active?

Like a mother, Shada felt teary, but she held it in. "I'm not sure what to say," she admitted. "When? Last night?"

"No, days ago, when—"

"When you collapsed." Shada ground her teeth. The rage she had felt against Damen resurfaced.

Marisa must have sensed it. She reached out to Shada and grasped her hands. "Don't be mad, Shada. Just listen, okay? Can you do that?"

Shada rolled her eyes. "Fine, go ahead."

Marisa sat back. "I'm sorry I lied to you."

"We always tell each other the truth."

"I know." Guilt colored the eyes Shada loved more than any others. "I'm sorry. Damen and I did go to the bowling alley, but then we realized I can't bowl. We had a good laugh, and he asked me what I wanted to do."

"Then he dragged you to his apartment?"

Marisa frowned at Shada, and Shada fell silent. She had promised to listen.

"*I* suggested we go to his place."

Shada refused to believe her.

"I did, Shada. I knew I could seduce him."

"You're kidding."

Marisa's face fell. "Are you saying a man wouldn't want me?"

"Of course not, sis. You're beautiful. Plenty would. I'm just saying it's hard to believe you would set out to get a man in bed."

Marisa grinned, appearing proud of herself. "Well, I did. He was hesitant at first, but I was determined."

"Oh, Marisa."

"I don't regret it, Shada. I lost my virginity. I'm finally a woman."

Shada couldn't help but laugh. "You've been a woman for years now."

"Agewise, but now I've had my rite of passage to lose my virginity."

"Isn't that more of a male thing?"

"It's for everyone," she declared and laughed.

She appeared more relaxed now that she had shared her secret. Shada could at least be satisfied with that. Marisa did seem more womanly right then, but it could be all in Shada's head.

"He was gentle and considerate, and now that I've had time to rest, I can look back at it with fond memories."

Shada snorted. "Fond, huh? I don't remember my first time being anything to describe with that word."

Marisa raised her chin, her eyebrows arched in superiority. "That's because I had mine with a man. You did it with a fumbling boy."

"Touché." Shada hugged her. "I just don't like you getting hurt, sis."

Marisa gave her a light squeeze and leaned back. "I know, but I wanted to do at least one thing all women do, something normal, before I die."

A sharp pain arrowed through Shada. "Don't talk like that. You're going to be around a long time."

"Do you understand how I feel, Shada?"

"Of course."

And she did. Everyone had desires, and Marisa's sickness didn't lessen hers for intimacy and the attentions of a man. Shada had always protected her sister, but most of the men Marisa had ever met either hightailed it when they found out she was sickly, or tried to take advantage of her. Shada ran off the losers, but she had failed to keep Damen away. The more she thought about what they had done, the more she began to think maybe it was good that Marisa had had the experience and that she didn't regret it.

That didn't mean Shada wouldn't skin him when she saw him. She had enjoyed the bruise she left on his face and suffered with satisfaction the swollen hand she'd got from clocking him.

Shada stood up. "I have a morning meeting, so we better get moving. In fact, I'm probably going to be late."

"I'm sorry for keeping you."

Shada walked to the refrigerator and opened the door. "Don't worry about it. You'll always come first." She froze and then leaned around the door to glare at Marisa. "You used protection, didn't you?"

Marisa blushed. Now the woman had the nerve to show embarrassment. "Yes, we did."

"Good. No babies for us."

———

Shada sat across from Creed, holding a coffee between her hands. She wasn't a big fan of coffee unless she had made the concoction herself, sweetening it and adding flavors that all but disguised the coffee taste. Pointless, so she didn't drink it often, except on days like today when she had had little sleep. The caffeine did nothing to calm her nerves, as if it could. Instead, they were jangled into a tight mess, and she wished to be anywhere other than across from the man who brought her body alive in ways she had only imagined. Things might be about to get a lot more complicated. *And what's complicated for me?* She had no idea what she wanted him to say or what she hoped he *wouldn't* say.

Unlike Marisa earlier, Creed seemed to be relaxed. His crisp white shirt lay open at the throat, giving her a glimpse of his smooth, hairless chest. She liked that about him and recalled the feeling of his hot, taut skin beneath her fingers. No one could deny she was attracted to him. *At least I haven't fallen in love with him.*

She started at the thought and shifted in her seat. A gulp of coffee burned her tongue, and she frowned. "Are you going to tell me what this is about?"

"First, I want to be straight with you," he said, meeting her gaze. "I want you in my bed regularly."

She licked her lips, her body growing hot. "Really?" Going for casual wasn't working.

"Yes, really. We're good together. You admit that, right?"

"Yeah, I'm not opposed to it."

He grinned, amused. "Good. I don't often meet a woman who likes my...darker side."

Shada smirked at him. "Darker, huh?" She leaned forward. "Are you into the BDSM lifestyle?"

His eyes widened, and he laughed. "No, nothing like that. Wait, are you?"

"No." She glanced around to see if they were being overheard. Most of the café's patrons were busy in conversations of their own or standing in line to place their order before they rushed back to work. "I like what you do to me. I like being spanked, and I like it rough. That's as far as I've ever gone, and I don't fantasize about more."

He nodded. "I don't meet a woman often who can take me like that." His gaze roved over what he could see of her body, and he lingered on her breasts. Shada was proud of them, their size and how they seemed to mesmerize Creed until he couldn't stop touching them. While she loved being dominated during sex with him, his weakness for her breasts gave her a sense of power she didn't mind.

"I have the same problem," she admitted. "You'd be surprised at how hard it is to find a man strong enough to handle me."

"Hmm." Her words seemed to please him. "We're in synch in that regard. So if I asked you to be my long-term lover, you would agree."

The words weren't a question, but she nodded anyway.

"However, I have another concern."

The butterflies were back. "What do you mean?"

"I need an heir."

She blinked at him. "Come again?"

"I want a child, someone I can leave my share of the corporation to."

Shada's mouth fell open. She had gone over various scenarios of what he might want to talk to her about, and she expected a discussion on them continuing as lovers. Never this. "A baby?"

"Yes, I want a baby."

Fear closed her throat, and she pushed the coffee away lest she choke on it with the next sip. "I'm not having your baby, Creed."

Surprise registered on his handsome face. She didn't know if it had to do with her presumption that he was asking her to have his baby, or if he didn't expect her to deny him.

"I wasn't asking you to have my baby, Shada."

"Well, why are you telling me about it?" she snapped.

He took her hand, but she jerked out of his hold.

"I didn't mean it that way." He spread his hands in supplication. "I meant, I wouldn't *presume* to think you were open to it."

She calmed down, and her hurt feelings settled. Getting hurt over the misunderstanding in the first place made no sense.

"I think I'm handling this wrong."

She couldn't help him and just sat waiting for him to choose his approach.

"First, tell me why you don't want children."

She shifted in her seat and glanced out the window. He was asking a question she wasn't comfortable getting into. "Not everyone wants children."

"Shada." He touched her hand. This time she didn't pull away. "If we're going to continue, we have to be honest with one another."

Continue what? she wondered. "When I was thirteen, my parents died in a car wreck. I was at school, and I remember what it felt like when the school counselor came personally to my classroom to get me. We walked together on the school grounds, just talking about my life and family. I thought it was odd, but hell, I was in math at the time and was glad to get out of there. After a while, we came back inside, and I thought she was going to let me return to class, but she took me into her office. That's when she told me the news that destroyed my world."

Creed laced his fingers with hers, and she drew from his strength. "I'm sorry, baby."

Why did it ache so good when he called her baby?

"What happened then?" he coaxed.

"I went into foster care, because I didn't have any other family. I was an only child, a spoiled only child, who was close to my parents. They were like my best friends, and they were gone. I thought I would die, and I had nothing to live for."

His grip tightened on hers.

"Then I met Marisa. She was eight, sickly, and her parents neglected her. She was so smart and happy, despite her circumstances. It got on my last nerve." Shada laughed. "I started taking care of her just because it seemed wrong not to. Right away, she started calling me her sister, and I appeased her by getting into the habit of calling her sis. Eventually, I loved her as much as I had loved my parents. So you see I don't want children."

He frowned. "People can love more than one person, Shada."

She sputtered, amused, and then grew serious. "I know that. I meant... I can't—I *won't*—expose a child to the kind of pain I experienced back then. If something were to happen to me when he is young, he'll be all alone. The thought of it kills me inside. I just can't do it."

"Shada."

"I know my reason is weird, and it makes no sense."

"No, I respect your decision and understand it, even if I don't agree. You also had the feeling reinforced by seeing what Marisa went through."

She had thought of that too, like what would have happened to Marisa if she had never come to their household, or if Marisa was a foster child. There were plenty of nightmarish experiences in the world, and maybe it wasn't logical to think the same thing that happened to her parents could happen to her. Yet knowing the truth had never changed her decision. She never wanted to get married or to have children. She never wanted to fall in love at all.

"So you're not asking me to have your baby. What are you saying?"

"I'm saying I want you to keep seeing me."

She blinked at him. "I know you aren't asking me to cheat on your wife with you, because that will get you a black eye to match your brother's chin."

He chuckled. "Damen will never live that one down. No, I'm not asking you to commit adultery. I don't plan on getting married either."

She gasped. "In vitro?"

He hesitated. "No, I don't want to trust my son or daughter to a lab. I want to find someone to have the baby, someone I can get to know. Ideally, she would be involved in the baby's life as his mother."

Shada shook her head. This was the way rich people thought? She didn't get it, but like he didn't judge her, she wouldn't judge him. Creed had a right to do what he wanted with his life, and from what she knew, he was a good man. He loved his brothers. He would probably be a good father. The thought threw her, and she pushed it away.

"Shada, I'm asking if you will consider continuing to be with me, if I'm honest with you and with the mother of my child. I won't have a relationship with her. I'll get her pregnant, but you alone will share my bed for our mutual pleasure."

His proposal was the most unorthodox thing she had ever heard. On one hand, she wanted to just cuss him out and storm from the café. On the other, neither of them were looking for a real relationship or love, so what harm would it do? Then again, while Shada was sure he could find a woman to agree to his terms, there was no telling if she'd secretly think she could keep him. Not to mention all the other kinds of baby-mama drama that could develop in such a situation.

"I don't know. It seems risky," she said. "Not much for me, but a lot for you, because of who you are."

He agreed. "True. I can't say I've thought this all the way through yet. What I do know is I want you. I'm not willing to give you up yet."

Warmth spread through her system despite the matter-of-fact way he said the words. "Can I think about it?"

"You can."

"Good. Well, I have to go. I'll see you later at the restaurant."

She fled, shocked, confused, even excited for some stupid reason. Myriad thoughts swirled through her head, foremost of all being Creed's long-term lover and having exclusive rights to his body. *Well, not exclusive, and there's the problem!*

CHAPTER TEN

Shada strode along the walk with a lazy step. From the moment she passed through the arch into the French Market, the oldest market in the United States, her intention of getting in and out quickly faded away. Over the last few days, she had thought about what she and Creed discussed, but she still couldn't pin down her emotions and decide what was best for her. Granted, she wanted to be with him, but looking the other way while he got another woman pregnant didn't feel right. She still managed to feel used and a little betrayed.

Walking under the covered pavilion where she had bought fresh produce plenty of times for the restaurant and for home, she lost herself as she stopped by the booths where she could peruse locally crafted jewelry. She made sure to pick up authentic New Orleans spices, again for home and the restaurant, and stopped to listen to a live duo. One man played drums, and another held an odd instrument she had never seen before. Looking like a giant guitar but held in an awkward position at the front of the man's body, the instrument produced music reminiscent of steel drums. Of course, that was weird, considering he plucked strings. Either way, she loved the tone and melody, as it soothed her spirit.

Shada must have had a questioning look on her face, because a woman with a friendly smile walked over to her. "It's called a kora," she explained, pointing toward the instrument Shada had wondered about. "A West African version of the harp and guitar."

"Wow, I had no idea," Shada said. "He plays it well, and the music it makes is incredible."

"I think so too." The woman went on to share a few more tidbits of trivia with Shada, and then she drifted away. Learning about the instrument, the history behind it, and the woman's friendliness were further reasons to love New Orleans.

Farther on, she stopped cold, staring at the man before her. She hadn't seen Damen since shortly after she had punched him, but here he stood at the French Market with a little girl. Neither had spotted Shada yet.

About seven, with dark hair down her back and almost black eyes, the girl pointed at a doll wearing a Mardi Gras mask. "Get me that, Daddy."

Shada started. Daddy? No one had said he had a child, and they had all worked together for a few months now. She hadn't seen the girl either. Granted, Damen flew back to New York regularly, just like Creed and Stefan, but still, he lived in New Orleans more often than not.

"Nita, I've bought you three already, and one is similar to that one. Plus you have a room full of dolls at your mom's house."

"So what?" The little girl's voice rose. "I want that one. You said you would buy me whatever I want. That's what I want, so get it for me. Now, Daddy, now!"

Oh no she didn't just stomp her feet and take that kind of tone with her father.

Shada waited for Damen to spank her ass or at least smack her lips for speaking to him that way.

"Fine, this is the last one," he said with mild annoyance. "I mean it, Nita."

"'I mean it?' Are you serious?" Shada tried to bite her tongue, but it was too late. Both Damen and Nita turned to her. She strode over to them. "You're going to let your daughter talk to you like that?"

Damen cast her a wary glance. She didn't blame him. Last time, she'd belted him. While she knew nothing about kids, she wouldn't humiliate him like that in front of his daughter.

Nita looked up at her, and Shada caught a glimpse of Marquette in the cheekbones and jaw. That was all, because it was obvious Nita was mixed. She looked Mexican, but with paler skin. "Do you know her, Daddy?"

"Hello, Shada," he said. "Yes, we work together. Nita, this is Shada. Shada, my daughter, Nita."

"I didn't know you had a child."

"She's been with her mother for the summer."

His words took her by surprise. Nita lived with Damen full time? "Let me guess. She comes back giving you attitude after every visit?" she asked.

He appeared embarrassed. "It's hard on her."

"Doesn't excuse disrespect, Damen."

"I should get going. See you later at Marquette's."

"Sure."

She let him go but noticed he didn't buy the doll. Rather, he practically dragged Nita along as she fussed and complained about how unfair it was. Shada wondered if this would be how Creed's child would end up when he found a mother. Well, it was none of her business. She should focus on her and hers, and nothing else.

With thoughts of Creed in mind, she finished her shopping and headed back to her apartment. After she had prepared lunch for Marisa and showered and changed clothes, she headed out again for the restaurant. Today, she determined, she would figure out what to tell Creed and let the chips fall where they may—whether it was to share her amazing lover for a little while or cut ties with him completely. The third choice was one she didn't allow herself to dwell on for more than thirty crazy, scary seconds.

The restaurant was packed, with every table filled, and Creed had booked a private room as well, so they were busy. In fact, he had arranged to bring on temporary staff to help in the kitchen and with serving. With the restaurant's success, now they had to take reservations and fewer walk-ins. Shada loved the place jumping the way it was, because she worked fine under pressure. What she didn't always appreciate were the constant interruptions, having to present herself to whatever self-important person had come in to dine with them.

"It's all a part of the chef's job," Creed had informed her, and she'd glared at him in response. As she passed ahead of him for the fourth time that evening, he touched her lower back, and chills of delight danced through her system. She craved him, but he hadn't said anything for several days except when it came to work. Neither had she, though, and she knew he waited for her decision.

"I need less of this part of my job and more standing over a hot stove, so to speak."

She didn't believe the look of sympathy he gave her when she peered at him over her shoulder.

"What about Rene?" she demanded.

Creed nodded toward the opposite side of the room. "He's been out here twice as much."

She rolled her eyes.

They arrived at the table, and Shada offered her best smile to the man who stood to shake her hand.

"You're Shada Howard?" he asked, and pleasure lit up the baby blues trained on her. He wasn't bad looking, with a thick-set, somewhat hard-looking body. His hair was thinning on top, which she could tell because she was inches taller than him.

"Yes, is that a problem?" She inserted a bit of teasing in her tone without thinking about it.

"Not at all. Arturo Benoit."

He held her hand a little too long. At her side, Creed cleared his throat, but she ignored it. How many women had simpered over him when he charmed them? Of course, he never crossed the line, and she wasn't the type to go crazy with jealousy. After all, they weren't a couple.

In the middle of this extended justification inside her own head, someone called Creed away, and he hesitated as if he wanted to stay close by. In the end, he had to tend to his duties.

"So, Shada," Arturo said. His smile seemed aimed to charm her, but all she thought about was how he kept her from her job. "How does a beautiful woman as young as yourself become head chef at such a prestigious restaurant?"

She tilted her head to the side and studied him. "Two things. I'm not as young as you think, and I'm not head chef."

His eyebrows rose toward his hairline. "Oh?" Somehow it rang false. "In that case, I can steal you away. I'm sure you have dreams of being on top."

"Who are you?"

"I told you. I'm Arturo Benoit. My restaurant has been in business since the eighteen hundreds. We're looking for a new head chef, and I've had my eye on you. I want you, Shada, and I'll give you whatever you want in order to have you."

Her jaw went slack. Was he serious? Right here, in the competition's dining room? He came to try to lure her away from Marquette's? Wow, the man had balls. Before she could formulate a reaction to this phenomenon, she was bumped aside and found herself looking at the broad back of one angry Creed Marquette.

"She's taken," he growled, getting into Arturo's face.

Shada darted out from behind Creed and grabbed his arm. "Hold on, Creed. You're making it sound like… Well, hell, so did he, but…"

Both men ignored her. Creed glanced down at the table where Arturo had finished his meal. "In fact, it looks like you're done. Good night."

Arturo drew himself up to his full height and still didn't meet Creed's chin, but the man was stocky. He raised his voice a couple of unnecessary decibels. "Is this how you treat your guests, Marquette?"

"*Guests* are invited and welcome," Creed shot back. "You're neither."

Shada thought she felt a stiff breeze at his words. Arturo's face grew beet red, and she spun to see where Stefan or Damen were. Then she spotted one of the men Creed had told her early on were there to assist him and his brothers. She had never paid them any mind, because they seemed to fade into the background. One of them, a hulking man as tall and as intimidating as Creed, stepped up to them.

"Is everything okay, Mr. Marquette?"

Shada had never heard anyone call Creed by anything other than his first name. Creed didn't take his eyes off Arturo, but he forced a wintery smile. "Mr. Benoit is leaving. His check is on us. Will you see him out, Pete?"

"Of course."

At last, it dawned on Shada what Pete and his companions were. They were bodyguards, and it made sense. While Creed and his brothers were muscular enough to look like they could handle themselves, they didn't want to focus on it while they went about their daily lives. Since it had come out that they were billionaires and their pictures had been shown in Forbes magazine, who knew how many people might target them. The thought scared her, and yet they worked almost daily in the restaurant, interacting with regular people.

Arturo preceded the bodyguard out. She didn't blame him, because the man looked like he wouldn't mind breaking a body in half. While she watched them head for the exit, she heard Creed snap his fingers. A busboy appeared and began clearing off the table. Creed pivoted toward her and took her arm.

"Creed, I have to get back to the kitchen."

"We're going to the kitchen," he quipped.

"I can get there under my own steam. Thanks."

He kept a firm hold on her elbow, and when they entered the kitchen, he kept them moving down the hall to his office. Once they were inside, he kicked the door shut and faced her.

Shada folded her arms over her chest. "Don't get an attitude with me. I didn't ask him to make me an offer. I didn't even know he existed before tonight."

Creed said nothing. He stood there staring at her.

"Will you say something or let me get back out there?"

She found herself thrust against the door, his hand at her throat, a thumb grazing her lips. Not a punishing touch, but a desperate one, as if he hadn't been able to resist caressing her skin. Creed followed with his body, aligning it with hers. He flicked up her chin to nuzzle her neck, and he moaned as he breathed in her scent.

"C-Creed." Her body came to life with a scorching need to be taken right there.

He slanted his lips over hers and seared her soul while he thrust his tongue into her mouth. Shada moaned and wrapped her arms around his waist. She felt his cock, so tight and thick against her belly. If she could just get him inside for a minute, the ache would ease.

She broke away and pushed at his chest. "We can't do this now."

"I know." With obvious reluctance, he dropped his hands to his sides and stepped back.

"What that guy said made you mad." Talk about stating the obvious.

Creed shrugged. He adjusted his cock to make it less noticeable in his pants. She grew hotter watching but forced her gaze to his face.

"You know he was offering me a job, right? Not to get into his bed?"

Creed's eyes flashed fire. "If he did, I would have ripped his head off, not just thrown him out."

A warm and cozy feeling came over her. "You still acted like it."

He swore. "What do you want me to say, Shada? I've already told you, you belong to me. Until you say otherwise, I'm not going to allow some idiot to make thinly veiled propositions to you. Period."

Now she grew angry. "Oh, that's rich. You're asking me to let you fuck another woman to get her pregnant!"

"You're not volunteering to be my baby's mother," he shot back.

The ridiculousness of the argument came through to her, but she was too pissed to stop. "You know what? I'm made my decision. We're done. I'm sure you'll have a nice, greedy candidate or a hundred before you know it."

"Shada."

She wrenched the door open and strode through it. As she walked back to the kitchen, tension in her shoulders made them ache, and a pain started in her chest. She expected any second he would grab her arm and drag her back to the office. He didn't follow. *I guess we're really done.*

For the rest of the night, Shada focused on work, keeping her head down. The few times she looked up and spotted Creed, she found him watching her, his expression unreadable. After hours, she was honored for a dessert sensation, and it meant a lot to her. Yet unhappiness kept surfacing to confuse her. She was getting everything she had ever wanted, and even Marisa seemed stronger. Her sister had been able to come to the celebration. Best of all, she and Damen weren't able to get into each other's pockets, not with Damen battling his spoiled daughter all evening.

Shada left the restaurant with Marisa at her side. She'd had much to think through, and she came to a firm understanding that she did what was right for her. Creed Marquette could kiss her ass.

CHAPTER ELEVEN

W here is Tiffany?" Creed boomed, and Shada swore the glasses rattled.

She'd seen him angry and irritable plenty of times. Most of it hadn't been aimed at her. Hell, she might have welcomed an argument the way they tiptoed around each other, Creed's smile so damn fake and her with a queasy stomach at the thought of seeing him one second and wanting to be in his arms the next. They managed through three weeks this way, and she hated it. The problem was that, despite her decision and his acceptance of it, what lay between them was still white-hot. She didn't need anyone to tell her that much when she caught Creed watching her, the fake cordiality stripped away. The first time had sent her running for the exit, mumbling about needing spices they already had in stock. Maybe she should call Arturo and take him up on his offer.

"Tiffany's out sick, remember?" Damen groused at his brother's question. "Probably from your temper. "Whatever's eating you, squash it, because you're fucking getting on my nerves."

Several snorts turned into coughs throughout the kitchen.

Creed glared at them all. "Really, Damen? Perhaps you called the agency for replacements when I asked you to, then? I think I remember you saying you could play manager for a day while I flew to New York?"

Damen reddened, then rounded on Creed. "I offered to go instead of you!"

Creed said something cutting in return, and Shada began to worry the brothers would come to blows. She took a step toward them when Stefan burst through the kitchen door. "Ladies, this is hardly the time. We have guests arriving in seconds."

Creed scowled at being called a lady, and Damen didn't appear to like it any better.

Served them right, she decided and undid her apron. "How about this? I'll help serve. I'm not even due in today, so I can be an extra set of hands."

"That's not your place," Creed said with a little less heat than he had given to his brother.

She strode by him, headed to the back, where there were a few extra serving uniforms. "I don't think it's *your* place, Creed, to tell me where I belong."

Another round of snorts.

"I'm your boss," he shouted after her, "or have you forgotten?"

"When I'm old, I hope my memory doesn't go like all of you people," Anita inserted into the void.

Shada stopped walking and looked back. When had the little girl arrived in the kitchen, and why hadn't Damen taught her some manners yet?

Damen rushed over to her. "Come on. You can order ice cream at your own table."

The two disappeared out the door, and Shada shook her head, then continued on to get changed. While she stood in the changing room unbuttoning her blouse, the door opened, and Creed stepped in. She clutched her blouse closed to hide her breasts.

"Creed! How about some privacy?"

His gazed skittered over her chest and held. Then he seemed to force it to her face. "You don't have to do this, Shada. I'll put a call in for help, and I'm sure I can get someone over here shortly."

"But they're not here now, and we have reservations and a private party to handle. Marquette's reputation is on the line."

He moved closer. She retreated a step.

"You care about the restaurant that much?"

"I…" She raised her chin. "While I'm here."

He frowned. "Are you planning to leave?"

"I'm not saying that. It's just that I like to give one hundred percent to whatever job I hold. You gave me a chance when no one else did, especially after my terrible first impression. I owe you."

His temper seemed to flame higher. "You don't have to stay because you feel you owe me something. I would never hold you back."

"Are you taunting me to leave?"

"I'm not. Trust me."

The man didn't understand. Yes, she could trust *him*, because he had never been anything but forthcoming with his desires and his expectations. What she couldn't trust was her reaction to him. Keeping Creed at arm's length was a daily challenge even when he didn't reach out for her like he started to do now.

At his movement, she teetered toward him. Her throat closed, her nipples pebbled, and all she had to do was topple into his embrace. He seemed to sense her struggle, and he reached out farther to encircle strong fingers around her wrist. A gentle tug brought her forward. Her hand fell from her blouse because she had no will to hold it, and Creed's gaze slid to her breasts. The black lacy bra might as well not be there, the way he stared.

"We don't have time for this," she murmured. "We said we were done."

"*You* said it."

"We can't," she tried again, her body now aligned with his, her head tilted back and lips parted to receive his kiss.

He lowered his head, and his lips were less than an inch from hers. She swallowed, feeling his warm breath, and her nostrils filled with his delicious manly scent. Beneath her palms, which she'd flattened on his chest, his heart beat. If he kissed her, she was gone. She squeezed her eyes shut and whispered, "Dragon."

Creed froze.

She waited for his mouth to descend onto hers, but where she had sensed his overwhelming presence a moment ago, it was now gone. Taking a peek, she found herself

CREED

alone, and the door tapped the wall as it swung wide. He had respected her use of their safe word. Why did it make her feel like crap?

Shada changed into a serving uniform and added the half apron the waiters and waitresses used. Then she headed out to the dining room. An hour of rushing to and fro had her feet aching, and she realized she covered much less ground working in the kitchen. True to his word, Creed managed to hire temporary staff, and she was relieved from duty.

Creed was still a bear, but he bit off the worst of the tirades. He ordered her to go home, and she took him up on it. She had never felt this far from him, as if a wall existed to keep them apart, even when she had first met him. Maybe it was just as well. Creed posed a danger to her equilibrium, and she apparently tempted the man night and day.

Walking home, she chuckled, thinking about her affect on Creed. *Let it go, Shada, and move on.* He was a great lover, but all good things ended. That was the hard lesson that life had taught her so far, and she would do well to remember it.

The balmy days had Shada feeling some type of way. She couldn't put her finger on it, but New Orleans's atmosphere was seeping into her bones. On the way to work, she paused to take in the sight of one of the voodoo shops, with its storefront window advertising charms, dolls, oils, candles, and brews. Through the glass, she spotted white shrunken heads hanging from wracks and a weird statue that looked like Medusa. A man with midnight-black hair reaching to his ass and matching clothing opened the shop's door to pass inside. Wasn't it a bit early for him? she wondered. A local news article she had read said vampires—people who liked to live the lifestyle of one of the undead—stalked this particular place.

She peered into the sky. For once the humidity gave her a break, but the sun shined bright.

Shada reached the restaurant and met Stefan on the street in front. "Hey, Stefan," she called. "What's up?"

The man who looked so like Creed, but with a heap less anger, smiled. *"Bonsoir, 'tit monde."* She winced at his lame Cajun French and the fact that *'tit monde* meant little one, which so did not describe her.

She patted Stefan's arm and smiled. "Give it up, Stefan. You can't get rid of that New York accent that easily."

His face fell, and she pressed a fist to her mouth to suppress a laugh.

"You wound me, Shada."

"Uh-huh."

They walked inside, and Stefan clapped his hands, his face lighting up with excitement.

"Why are you so happy?" she asked.

He winked and touched a finger to his lips. "Because our piano player is out tonight, and I didn't tell Creed."

She blinked at him. "Um, dude, you know your brother is going to kill you, right?"

He just smiled.

She shook her head and headed toward the kitchen. Who knew what Stefan was up to? However, she didn't believe he would do anything to screw with the well-oiled machine they had going. As she prepared for the evening guests, she thought about what Stefan had said and considered warning Creed. When Creed showed up for work with a bombshell of a woman, with legs from her throat to the floor, Shada decided he could suck it.

While Creed introduced the woman around, Shada moved to the back of the group. She caught Creed looking her way and spun on her heel to enter the kitchen. *Who's not jealous now? Shut up!*

During preparation, gossip swirled around her. "You think she's his new lover?" her junior cook asked the porter. He shrugged and widened his eyes with a pointed look at Shada. She turned away from both of them and pretended not to have heard.

So everyone knew she'd been sleeping with Creed. No one had treated her in a negative way because of it, except Tiffany, of course.

Was the woman a candidate to have Creed's baby? He *would* choose a beautiful white woman. She hated how the bitterness rose but couldn't help it. Her reaction said she had made the right decision to break it off with him. She wouldn't have survived being involved with him while he was trying to get another woman pregnant. The whole scenario just pissed her off every time she thought about it.

Music from the baby grand started up in the main dining room, and Shada dropped what she was doing with an order to her *commis* to cover for her. She darted through the door and found Stefan sitting at the piano, his long, masculine fingers flying over the keys with expertise. A smooth jazz piece lit the air and transformed the atmosphere. His skill was impressive, especially since Creed had said Stefan taught himself to play the guitar to be like their dad. Did he teach himself the piano as well?

The drummer they had hired not long ago joined Stefan, and they played well together, as if they had been practicing. Creed appeared in the kitchen doorway and frowned at his brother.

Shada couldn't help wandering over to him. "Did you recognize his playing?"

"No, someone told me."

Creed didn't look at her. He seemed to be debating whether to go over to chew Stefan out, but then his face cleared. For an instant, she caught a glimpse of the affection and favoritism both Creed and Damen showed Stefan. An instant later, his expression closed, and he peered down at her. Her heart had the nerve to skip a beat. Creed's gaze locked on hers and then slid to her lips. She stilled, feeling like she'd been caught in the sights of some wild animal. One false move, and she was a goner.

"You didn't meet—" he began.

She held up a hand. "You're not that ignorant."

He shoved his hands into his pockets. "I'm not doing anything to hurt you, Shada."

"As if you could," she shot back and returned to the kitchen. He didn't call after her, and that hurt too. A dawning realization came over her, but she refused to believe the truth of it.

The evening continued without incident. Stefan entertained all night with his playing, taking short breaks here and there at Creed's insistence. At last, the staff was alone to clean up and do the prep work for the next day. Shada wondered where the blonde had gone, but no one said.

Music from the dining room caught her attention only because a deep baritone had joined in. "No way," she whispered and left her task again. As before, Creed stood near the kitchen, arms folded while he listened to his brother sing.

"Wow," she said, coming up beside him. "He's got a great voice. I can see why he wanted to go pro. I mean he'd have had the women eating out of his hand."

Creed made a rude noise, and she laughed. "Are you jealous?"

"Of?"

She shrugged and grinned.

Stefan finished the jazz piece he'd been playing and started a new song with a familiar soulful beat. "Come and join me, Damen."

Damen glanced over at Creed, grinned, and abandoned the chairs he had been stacking. He pulled an electric guitar out from somewhere she hadn't noticed and hooked it into speakers.

Shada slapped a hand over her mouth, eyes wide. She turned to Creed, about to burst. "Are they seriously singing the blues?"

Creed groaned. "Yes, they are."

"I know that song. Oh my goodness, they actually sound like they know what they're doing."

The kitchen door opened, and every single staff member piled into the dining room to listen and watch as

Stefan and Damen sang together. A few laughed and clapped their hands. Shada joined in. She couldn't believe the Marquette brothers were both sexy and talented. Men must be weeping all over the globe.

"Hey, Creed," Stefan shouted above the music.

Shada glanced at Creed, whose face had turned to stone. She pressed her lips together to keep from laughing, and when she had pulled herself together, she leaned closer to him. "Aren't you going to sing?"

His jaw worked, but he said nothing. Stefan kept signaling to him, and a few others picked up on it and began spurring Creed to get out there. Shada recalled the time Creed told her they sang for their food on the streets of New York. From his telling, she had assumed they sounded a mess, and people gave them money because they were cute teenage boys. Stefan and Damen's voices blended well, and they picked up on each other's cues with ease. Of course, they weren't perfect, but that added to their charm. Then there was Creed, who, judging by the flare of his nostrils and the arrogant fire in his eyes, wouldn't be caught dead singing with his brothers at his age.

Shada touched Creed's arm and smirked. "I guess you're scared."

His eyes blazed. "I'm not afraid."

She shrugged. "Hey, it's nothing to be ashamed of. We're all scared of something, and I mean, maybe you're not as good as they are. This is your restaurant. Sure, it's after hours, and all the guests are gone. But these people cheering your brothers on are your staff, and you can't look bad in front of them."

He grumbled, and then a hand snaked out and drew her closer to him. She gasped and tried to get away. He held on. The man turned the tables on her.

"Creed, stop. Everyone will—"

"Come home with me tonight, and I'll sing."

She did her best to straighten so her nipple—which had pebbled from the second she came into contact with his chest—wouldn't be apparent to him. "My pussy is not for trade."

His stubborn gaze challenged her.

"I thought we weren't doing that anymore."

"Says you."

The words *you've already found somebody new* hovered on her lips, but she wouldn't stoop to speaking them aloud.

"Not a good idea, Creed." She felt her resistance crumbling and hated that she was being a bad example to all women, even if they didn't know her or the situation.

"Tonight," he said.

In other words, he wanted her once more. Damn, how many times had they slept together with the intention of making it the last time? She hadn't let him touch her for three weeks now, and her body cried out for mercy. Maybe he had been getting fulfillment all along, never missing a beat when he replaced her with the leggy chick.

She turned back to watch Stefan and Damen. "Maybe I'll go up there and sing myself."

Creed was smart enough to know she tried to use reverse psychology on him, but she'd also issued a challenge of her own. She stepped just ahead of him and cheered with more enthusiasm, acting as if she would continue toward the front, but Creed's hands came around her waist, and he set her aside. He weaved through the tables, and her excitement leaped a hundred feet higher when she saw him walk up to stand beside Damen. Although there was a slight pink to his cheeks, he stood tall and exuded sexiness. From the moment Creed opened his mouth, Stefan lowered the volume of his playing, and both brothers stopped singing to give Creed the lead. Several of the young women screamed at Creed's soulful tones, and Shada put a hand to her chest. Creed wasn't a better singer than Stefan, but he was damn good.

As he sang about love lost and misunderstood, he scanned the crowd. His gaze lit on her and held. Her heart stuttered to a stop and then kick-started with a vengeance. Tempted to pant, she breathed deeply and couldn't look away from him. A couple more songs, and the brothers called it a night. Shada added her compliments to those of the workers swarming around the brothers and then escaped to the kitchen. She kept her distance from Creed for the rest of the night and then hightailed it out of there when he entered his office. Yes, she acted like a scared rabbit, but damn it, at least she didn't give in to him. That was the important thing, and she concentrated on recalling every detail of the impromptu concert—for Marisa's sake, of course.

CHAPTER TWELVE

What were you thinking, Creed?"

Creed grumbled and stared at the words swimming before his eyes. "Fuck off, Damen."

His brother parked on the edge of his desk. "What was her name? Gwendolyn?"

Creed swore. "Madeline."

Damen frowned. "Not a fan."

"Shut the hell up!"

"Why are you so grumpy this morning?" Damen reached for the empty bottle on the edge of the desk. "Did you polish off all of this? No wonder you're being an ass. Bet that head feels good, huh?"

Creed had been trying to ignore the pounding in his head and the cotton on his tongue. Leave it to Damen to be in the mood to rib him today, when he could kill anything that moved. A few nights ago, Shada had run out on him, and she wouldn't answer his calls. He'd gotten the message through Damen that she was taking time off. He had never met an employee in the years he and his brothers had run their corporation who flouted authority more than Shada. Yet he had put up with it. Why?

Because I...

He clamped down on his thoughts and ran a hand over his face. "Why the hell did she call you to tell you she wasn't coming in and not me?"

Damen grinned. "We were discussing Melody, not Shada."

"Madeline!" Creed groaned at the loudness of his own voice. "Look, you know I've been thinking about it for a while. I'm thirty-five. I want a child."

"Don't worry. You don't have eggs to go bad. You're good to maybe ninety."

Creed stared at his brother. Despite his foul mood, he wanted to laugh. He cracked a smile, and Damen slapped a hand on his shoulder, sending an explosion through his head. All humor fled.

"That's better," Damen said, oblivious to his pain or perhaps unsympathetic. "So you grabbed some woman off the street and asked her to let you fuck her to get her pregnant. She said yes, and Shada's the one that's screwed. Well, so to speak."

"I didn't screw Shada. We're not... We didn't agree on the terms I set."

"Terms you set? Whoa, my big brother is a prick. I always knew it."

"Damen," he warned.

"Just trying to understand why you're drowning yourself in a bottle. You don't drink, Creed."

"I've tried it before."

"Yeah, once. I'm surprised you're not under the table, but then this is only wine."

Damen's worry started to seep through. Damen and Shada had talked about fear the night he and his brothers sang, but the one thing he did fear more than any other was becoming like his dad. Damen and Stefan knew that about him and never tried to get him to let go and drink with them. Neither, as far as he knew, had a problem, but the three of them understood the risks.

"So why now?" Damen continued.

"Don't try getting inside my head, Damen. Let it go. I gave in to what you and Stefan wanted. You should be happy."

"This isn't about the restaurant. Even if you won't admit it, you're happier here in New Orleans, Creed. Maybe we weren't meant for the corporate life."

Creed scowled. "You want to give the money back now?"

"I didn't say that. I remember those nights when—"

"Yeah." Creed didn't want to revisit the past.

"We're not doing too bad, and Stefan's got an idea for—"

"No!"

Damen chuckled. He raised his hands as if in defense. "I was going to say for a foundation, somewhere to dump our money where we can do good for kids that are in the situation we were in."

Creed admitted this wasn't a bad idea, but he wouldn't yet accept that the corporate life wasn't for them. He did like the restaurant business, maybe even loved it, with its hectic pace and constant challenges. They gave him a rush in a way. At least he never found himself fighting to keep his eyes open in meetings with pompous blowhards. Not in New Orleans.

"And you've got to admit *she* makes it fun for you."

"There is no she," he snapped.

"Not if you're going to cheat on her."

"Fuck, Damen, I told you she's not my woman." He recalled the times he had asserted Shada was his, and he shoved the papers on his desk away from him. Maybe he should go over there and demand she speak to him. No, he couldn't do that. Shada drove him insane. He wanted to wash his hands of her and move forward with his plan. Yet he also wanted to spank her for running away from him, along with a few other things. *No, it's more than that...* He surged to his feet, cutting off the thought.

His brother smirked at him. "Why are you so pissed off?"

"I'm always pissed off. When have you known me not to be?"

"When Shada's making you smile."

"Fuck Shada!"

Something fractured in his mind. He stormed toward the door, wrenched it open, and slammed it behind him as he left. Nausea assailed Creed as he left Marquette's and took to the streets. Making his point had cost him, and all he wanted was his bed, but lying at home alone hadn't done him any good when he was there. He'd lain awake most of the night for the last two days, unable to sleep. She wouldn't leave his thoughts, and worse, he worried about her. Would she leave the restaurant to go work for another? Would she take a new lover? He had no right to wonder. He knew that, because he hadn't been fair to her. Never in his life had he cheated on a woman, and he didn't feel like his proposal to her was cheating. He'd been up front and given her a choice, but it was still selfish. He acknowledged that. Yet he couldn't see himself giving up the idea of having a baby.

They weren't meant for each other. The truth stared him in the face, but he had a hard time accepting it.

"Maybe I've had my way too long, and I don't know how to handle it now." He ignored the looks he got from others walking along in the early morning. One couldn't say he always got his way, when Damen and Stefan made a daily habit of defying his wishes. In fact, he began to think they looked for ways to thwart him. As he considered Marquette's and now this idea of starting a foundation, he wondered if perhaps he'd been living a lie all along. He might be just some guy trapped by his past, and his brothers the ones who drew him out. "And Shada."

Creed swore. There she was, popping into his head again. He stopped walking and looked to his left. Thick white columns lined the walk and supported the overhanging roof above. To his right, green doors with long windows allowed him to see into the famous café he had visited many times during his stay in New Orleans. Café du Monde was known for its beignets and café au lait, and Creed had enjoyed the puffy fried dough with piles of powdered sugar on top coupled with the hot coffee that was half milk. He'd propositioned Rene to try the treat for

Marquette's and had been told one couldn't improve on perfection. Shada, he recalled, had laughed at him, and then, when he grumbled about dealing with arrogant chefs, she had promised to create something unique to Marquette's. He swore. There she was again in his head. When his cell phone rang, he welcomed the interruption, at least until Shada's name flashed on the screen.

Creed battled between letting her call go to voicemail and finding out what she'd been doing all this time since she had finally decided to call him. A desire to hear her voice outweighed his anger, and he answered. "Shada, perhaps you forgot you have a job to do."

"Creed."

The anguish in her tone tore through him. "What is it, baby?"

"She's gone. She's *gone*."

Her sobs ripped him apart. He didn't need the details. All he needed was to find her and take her into his arms.

"Where are you?" he demanded.

For a few moments, she couldn't answer, and he paced with the phone pressed into his ear until it hurt. At last, she mumbled, "Home."

"Don't move. I'll be there."

The apartment Shada shared with her sister was within walking distance of Marquette's, but Creed had covered a lot of ground in the opposite direction when he left the restaurant. He doubled his speed and considered getting public transportation, but thought better of it. Pent-up frustration and worry gave him enough energy to get to Shada under his own steam. Besides, he needed to get his blood pumping and to work out his hangover so he could concentrate on her.

While he walked, Creed searched with his phone's browser for the name of the management company where Shada lived. From that info, he obtained the phone number and dialed them. A woman with a heavy accent came on the line, but living in this city for the time he had, he understood her without a problem.

"This is Creed Marquette. I need someone to meet me at Unit Three on St. Philip to let me into the apartment."

"Are you the tenant, sir?"

"No, I'm her employer. I will be there in—"

"I'm sorry, Mr. Marquette. If your name isn't on the lease, we can't let you in without the tenant's written consent."

His patience snapped. "Listen, Shada Howard, the tenant, is in a...precarious state right now. I'm not sure she's in the frame of mind to answer the door. So I want someone there to let me in, just in case. If that person wants to come inside with me to ensure I'm not about to commit foul play, that's fine. However, I will enter that apartment, with your assistance or without."

"Mr. Marquette, it don' matta what you say. Ah cane't let you in." The angrier she grew, the thicker her accent, and he had to concentrate to understand. "Now if you're going to threaten us in this way, I will have to call the police."

"Please do, if you must, but have someone with a key for the door," he shot back. "I will be there in twenty minutes."

He disconnected the call, and just as he said he would, he arrived outside Shada's apartment twenty minutes later.

When he started up the stairs toward unit three, he found an older gentleman standing beside the door, waiting. Creed saw no evidence of the police, and he sighed in relief. While he had no doubt he could settle matters with the authorities quickly, he didn't need the delay in getting to Shada.

"You're Creed Marquette?" the elderly man asked in a gruff tone.

"I am," Creed said, but he strode by the man to knock on Shada's door. He waited a few beats to see if she would answer, but he heard nothing from the apartment. "Open it."

"Well now, hang on," the old man said. "We need to—"

"Open it before I do."

An unsteady hand covered in age spots reached out to the door. The man pushed the key into the lock and turned it. Once the door opened, Creed brushed by the man even as he called out to Shada and announced himself. Creed rushed through the living room, shuffling footsteps sounding behind him.

"We would have called the police if Ms. Alma hadn't thought to look you up. Marquette name sounded familiar. Pretty well-known, you."

Creed ignored the conversation and turned into the first bedroom he reached. He found Shada there, crumpled at the side of the bed, her head and shoulders bowed. In the bed before her, Marisa lay as still as the dead, and he knew that was the case. She had passed on. Creed couldn't say the situation was unexpected, with Marisa always so weak, but it hit him hard. Marisa had been a sweet and intelligent woman, and he knew that, even if Shada wouldn't accept it, Damen had liked her. Maybe more than he should have.

For now, Creed dismissed everyone from his mind except the trembling beauty before him. He knelt down on one knee and scooped her into his arms. "No," came her weak cry, but she seemed to lack the strength to fight him. He carried her from the room and sat on the couch with her in a tight embrace.

"I need to stay with her," she whispered.

"Shada, baby, she's gone. She can't stay in the apartment. She has to be laid to rest."

"No, no, she's my sister."

"Shh, I know." He did his best to calm her with words, but in the end, all he could do was hold her tight.

She sobbed nonstop, shaking so much his heart threatened to crack. "I can't live without her, Creed. I just can't," she cried.

"It feels like you can't, baby, but I promise you it will get better." He stroked her hair and kissed the top of her head. She clung to him, and he willed some of his strength into her. "If you can't, I will help you. You can lean on me all you need to."

Shada buried her face against his chest, her fingers curled into his shirtsleeves. A sound made him look up, and he found the old man standing before him, confused. "Is that young lady in there really—"

"Be quiet," Creed roared. "I don't need you here anymore. Get out."

Shada, who had settled down some, started to cry again, and the old man stumbled to the door and disappeared.

Creed shifted Shada into a different position on his lap and maneuvered his phone from his pocket.

"Baby, I'm going to handle everything. You relax."

She didn't answer, and he made some phone calls. Within moments, he had arranged for the body to be picked up and informed his brothers. Stefan was on his way to bring meds for Shada to take. He knew she wouldn't sleep without help.

When he set his cell phone down, Creed stood Shada on her feet. "Come on, let's get you into bed." Before they had taken one step, her eyes widened and she stared toward the bedroom door. For an instant, Creed had thoughts of a lingering ghost, a popular belief here, but then he realized Shada feared breaking down again. He had the feeling she hadn't fully accepted Marisa was gone.

"On second thought, you're staying with me."

"Creed."

His name was her only protest, but he got her moving down to the street. Just as they stepped on the front walk, a car pulled up, and Damen unfolded from the interior.

Creed frowned. "Where's Stefan? She doesn't need to see you, Damen."

His brother appeared paler than usual. He didn't look at Creed but focused on Shada. "Shada, I'm sorry. I'm so, so sorry."

Creed knew his brother, and he heard the disillusionment in Damen's tone.

Shada stared at the ground, not meeting his eyes. Creed couldn't tell if she was angry at his brother or didn't hear him speak at all.

He held out his hand for the meds, and Damen handed them over. He could tell Damen wanted to say more, but he shook his head. "Give her time. If you could wait inside until…"

Damen nodded and backed off. Creed knew he asked for a lot, but Damen was stronger than Shada right now. He believed his brother would do what he could. Creed tucked Shada into the car and slid behind the wheel. He waved to both his bodyguard, who had dogged his steps the entire way over there, and to Damen. His brother would find his way back.

"She's staying with me. I'll be in later."

Damen leaned on the driver-side door and glanced across at Shada. Creed studied her beautiful face as well. Her hands were clutched in her lap, and her shoulders shook. His brother squeezed his shoulder. "Don't bother. We'll handle it. She needs you."

Creed agreed and pulled off. Now he had to figure out how to help Shada through the next few days, maybe even the next few weeks and months.

CHAPTER THIRTEEN

Creed stood behind Shada in the shower. Warm water ran over her bowed head, and he drew her toward him a little. He ignored the reaction in his body, which responded to her nakedness. Shada didn't need to think about sex right now, so he didn't. Despite his hard-on, he washed her, running a cloth over her soft skin, careful not to let his fingers touch it. Every now and then, she shuddered, and it tore at him.

"Spread your legs, baby," he encouraged her.

She didn't move, so he pushed a knee between her thighs to do it himself. Her heat warmed his hand, but he worked quickly. As he turned off the shower, he noted the mess of her hair, wondering what the heck he would do with it. He knew nothing of styling a woman's hair. Thoughts of calling in a stylist ran through his mind. She would need to come to him, because he wouldn't subject Shada to stepping out in public before she was ready. For now, he would dry her hair, wrap it, and get her into bed.

Creed tucked Shada beneath the sheets and brought in warm milk and the medicine. He held the glass out to her, but she shook her head.

"One sip for me," he encouraged her.

"It's gross."

He reached for her chin and tipped it up. "You haven't kept down anything that I gave you earlier. Drink enough to take your medicine, Shada." Instilling firmness in his tone got her to drink, but he hated doing it. He'd wanted to treat her tenderly in this terrible time. As he had watched her over the last twenty-four hours, he realized the shudders might occur when she recalled finding her sister. Add to that the memory of her parents being taken from her when she was so young, and Shada must feel she was all alone in the world. He determined to change that perception until she grew stronger.

She sighed and took the glass. She popped the pills into her mouth and then drank. When she'd taken two swallows, she pushed it away, and he set it aside. He tucked the sheets beneath her chin and turned away.

"Creed."

He froze at her small voice, as she hadn't spoken much since he'd picked her up, and he looked back at her.

"Stay with me. I can't be alone. I just can't."

He dropped to his knees at her bedside and stroked her cheek. "You're not, Shada."

"Please."

"You don't have to beg me. Hold on. Let me put something on."

He'd forgotten he stepped out of the shower naked, and he'd put her to bed without a stitch on herself. He couldn't lie in bed with her that way, so he found a T-shirt and shorts, then slipped behind her. She tucked her head beneath his chin and drew her knees to her chest. Creed enfolded her in his embrace and shut his eyes, resting while she did.

———

Shada sat up on the side of the bed, which woke Creed. He studied her beautiful face as she bowed her head. Concern washed over him. How long had it been since he'd given her something for the pain? Had enough time passed to give her more? Other than the pain, he could imagine what she felt. All she wanted was to disappear, but he had also begun to see some light. She acknowledged him and her surroundings more and more with each hour that passed. She would go on and beat this grief.

A buzzing caught her attention, and as she reached for his cell phone on the side table, he sat up and caught her hand. For a few moments, she blinked at him as if she couldn't clear her vision.

"Come back to bed, Shada."

She didn't move.

Creed stroked her face and then wrapped an arm about her waist to draw her to his chest. "Come on, baby."

"I'm hungry."

Her small voice provoked a protectiveness in him. He pushed her down against the mattress and drew up over her. "Okay, I'll make you food, but stay put."

Creed had the ingredients for a sandwich he knew Shada liked. Since arriving in New Orleans, she had learned to make and enjoy the Italian *muffuletta*, or muff for short. He had seen her put the creation together, and he felt confident he could recreate it. From the refrigerator, he removed muffuletta bread, olive salad, olive oil, salami, Italian ham, and provolone cheese. He cut the bread in half across the middle, brushed the halves with olive oil, and began layering the meat and cheese. On top, he added a healthy amount of olive salad, then smashed the whole together. With care, he placed the sandwich on a saucer, cut it, and prepared Earl Grey tea. When everything was ready, he took Shada's lunch in to her on a tray and presented it with a flourish.

Shada sat up as he approached the bed, her eyes widening at the sandwich.

He grinned. "Looks good, doesn't it? It's the muff."

"I see," she murmured.

He couldn't tell if her response was one of pleasure or something else. When he sat her lunch before her, he hovered, waiting. Somehow he was nervous. He'd dealt with people from all backgrounds, and he found that running a corporation came naturally once he had learned the ropes. Yet standing before this woman while she passed judgment on his creation took all his courage, and he didn't like it.

Shada raised one side of the sandwich a bit awkwardly and leaned forward. He realized she would never be able to open her mouth wide enough to reach from the top of the loaf to the bottom. She settled for the bottom section and chewed.

"Do you like it?" he asked, then cleared his throat because he sounded like a damn wuss.

"It's good," she said.

He heard a little something. "What did I do wrong?"

"Nothing."

"Shada."

She sighed. "I like some of the dough taken out of the middle so the bread's not so thick, and you were a little heavy-handed with the oil. Then there's—"

"I get it. I suck at cooking."

He reached for the plate, but she raised the sandwich to her lips and continued to eat.

"You don't have to force yourself, Shada."

She ignored him and finished the sandwich. After the last bite disappeared into her mouth, she climbed off the bed. He couldn't help allowing his gaze to follow her movements, enjoying the sight of her naked body as she went into the bathroom. The toilet flushed. Water came on at the sink. He heard her brushing her teeth and recalled how he had helped her do even that after he brought her to his home.

She appeared again, but this time she'd covered herself, wearing a robe he had left on the back of the bathroom door. The material hung well past her hands and almost to the floor. She seemed lost in it, and smaller. A pain tightened the muscles in his chest.

"Come back to bed," he encouraged her.

"I need to make arrangements."

"I've begun those," he said.

He started to explain to her that the dead in New Orleans are buried aboveground in vaults and that, because of a shortage in space, the body would only occupy its casket space for a short while before being transferred to a bag and placed in the back of the vault to make room for the next occupant. The casket would then be thrown away. When he had heard about the process, enacted because of an ordinance in New Orleans, he had been shocked beyond belief. He didn't want to share the details with Shada and wondered if they should just have Marisa's body shipped back to New York for burial.

"Metairie Cemetery?" she said, surprising him.

"You know about the customs here?"

She swallowed and nodded, but he saw how difficult it was for her. "Marisa learned everything there was to know about her new city and told me. She loved this place from the first moment our plane touched down. I'll lay her to rest here."

She wobbled, and he caught her so he could guide her to the bed to sit down. Creed dropped to one knee and cupped her chin in his palm. "I'll pay for everything."

"No, I—"

"It's settled, Shada."

She glared at him, but the expression faded right away. From the look of it, the death of her sister had sapped all her energy, and Shada couldn't fight his will in her current state. He knew he took advantage of it, managing what she hadn't turned over to him. She needed him, the decision had to be made, and he got it done. Period.

Over the next day or so, Creed stood with Shada, along with his brothers and a few of his employees, to say good-bye to Marisa. Creed held Shada while she cried against his chest. He witnessed her weakness and the point when she decided to stand on her own two feet. She dried the tears and raised her chin, but he noted the way she held onto his arm as he escorted her from the cemetery.

"You okay?" Damen asked as they neared Creed's car.

Creed glanced down at Shada beside him and back to his brother. "We're fine. You're..." He wasn't sure what Marisa had been to Damen, other than a brief lover. Damen hadn't confided in him, and Creed hadn't pushed, because he knew his brother could handle the loss. Shada had needed him.

Damen shrugged, but Creed saw a touch of sadness in his gaze before it disappeared. He started to say something, but Damen swung away and headed toward his own vehicle. Stefan joined him, and Tiffany hitched a ride with the two of them.

Creed tucked Shada into his vehicle and slid behind the wheel. When he started the car, she sighed.

He eyed her a second, judging her mood. "We can skip the celebration at the restaurant, if you like."

She turned a hopeful gaze on him. "That seems so wrong, but I just don't think I can do it. Do you think the others will mind?"

"No, they'll understand. If they don't..." He clenched his jaw, and she tried to smile but failed. Her small fingers curled around his when he took her hand. "I'll take you wherever you want to go."

"To your place," came the rapid response.

He hesitated.

"I want you to fuck me."

"Shada, I don't think that's a good idea with the state you're in. Remember, we broke it off before this happened."

"I know. Are you saying you don't want to anymore?"

His cock twitched at the sheer thought, and she questioned his desire. "I want you. I just don't want to take advantage of you. You're vulnerable right now. I'd be a sorry S.O.B. to take you to bed, feeling the way you do."

"It's *because* of the way I feel I want to." She twisted to face him as he idled rather than pull out into traffic. "She fills my thoughts. I can hear her laughter, see the twinkle in her eyes, even when she was at her lowest physically. It hurts so bad I can't breathe. If for an instant I can forget, I want it like a drug. Can you understand?"

He could. Still, he hesitated. If she should change her mind half way through or afterward and get angry at him for giving in to his weakness, then what would they do? The will to say no crumbled with each passing second, and he opened his mouth to tell her.

She rested her hand over his crotch and gave his cock a squeeze.

Damn! "Shada."

She rubbed his shaft until it hardened, then shifted in her seat until the form-fitting black dress she wore rose up her soft brown thighs.

Need robbed him of the ability to speak. The word *no* was the farthest it had ever been from his lips. Creed leaned across the seats, turned her chin up toward him, and claimed her mouth. She'd better not tell him no, he decided as he thrust out his tongue. Her soft moan tightened his cock even more, and he jerked away to force the car into gear. Fifty minutes later, they arrived at his house, and he pulled into the gravel drive.

Creed escorted Shada inside. Where he normally would have taken her the second they crossed the threshold, having ripped off every shred of clothing, he kept firm control of his desires until they reached his bedroom.

She tossed her purse on the settee and strode to the bed. Creed followed, watching the sway of her hips. His cock, which hadn't softened since she first touched it in the car, tented his pants and strained to be set free. He moved up behind her and lay his hands on her shoulders. Dipping at the knee, he brought his erection into contact with her round ass and almost moaned with pleasure. Shada arched her back and ground into him. All of a sudden, a desperate need to take her from behind came over him. They had had anal sex plenty of times, so he knew she liked it. He ached to possess her, but he wasn't sure if that was what she needed. Perhaps she longed to take it slow and easy.

When she pulled away from his grasp, Creed let her go with reluctance. With her back turned to him, Shada unzipped her dress and drew it over her shoulders. She stepped out of it and tossed it to join her purse. Black matching panties and bra met his gaze, made sexier by her bare legs and high heels. She flattened her hands on the bed and pushed out her ass again. Creed didn't have to guess what his woman asked him for. She was so in tune with his sexual desires, it was uncanny.

Creed dropped to his knees and ran his fingers over the lacy material of her panties. He thrust them aside and kissed one rounded cheek, then the other. Shada rocked her hips. He licked a finger and then thrust it between her crack to massage her anus. Her moan pleased him. A little bit of pressure got him past the barrier's edge, and he felt her tremble.

"Lean forward," he ordered, instilling gentleness in his tone.

She did as he asked. The fact that his bed was a high one allowed for her ass to be raised enough so he didn't have to bend down too much. He positioned himself to the side of her and leaned on the bed. Easing his finger deeper, he watched as he invaded her body, loving every second of it. She squirmed, and he liked it. Shada incited his passions even more when she pretended to try to escape him. Yet she couldn't help reacting to his touch. He loved that too, the way her pussy wept at the slightest manipulation of any one of her erogenous zones.

While he thrust his finger in and out of her ass, Creed spread her legs with a knee. He found the sight he'd been hoping for, come moistening her pussy lips and wetting the tops of her thighs. "Mmm, look what you have for me, baby."

"Creed, don't tease me." Her lips parted, and she shut her eyes.

He paused to stare at her. *Damn, she's beautiful and sexy. I can't get enough. I want all of her.*

"You like when I tease you," he said, and he twisted his hand so that his finger rotated in her ass. He pushed deep, and his palm met with her cheeks. A gentle squeeze and a wiggle had her scratching at the sheets. Creed leaned down to kiss her back while he worked her tight ass. Her anus pulsed around his digit, seeming to beg for more. He couldn't go deeper until he filled her with his cock. A desperate ache said to do it now, but he liked to torment himself, to drive his lust to stir-crazy mode. "Think about me, Shada. About how it's going to feel when I get my dick in you and fuck you hard. Is it going to hurt or feel good?"

"Both," she pleaded.

He grinned. "Is that what you want?"

"You know what I want, damn you!"

Mine. He kissed her back again while he worked his hand. The tiny noises she made caused his cock to twitch in his pants. *Wait a little longer.* He nipped at the spot just above her shoulder blade, then sucked the skin into his mouth. By the time he let go, the area was reddened. He licked it and gave it a kiss. She murmured softly and sweetly. His tolerance ended.

Creed pulled his finger from her ass and straightened. Shada complained, but she waited where she was, leaned over the bed. He shuffled out of his clothing, tossing away each article to land where it may. When he had removed his socks and shoes as well, he scrounged up a condom from the bedside table and rolled it into place. Lubricant, which he also kept on hand, coated her rear entrance. He dropped to his knees, spread her legs wide, and nosed in to eat her pussy, but he didn't stay long. His cock couldn't stand being outside her body much longer. He gave a through swipe at her cream and coated his tongue, then swallowed as he stood up. Shada begged him for satisfaction. He positioned himself behind her and' allowed the head of his cock to graze her anus.

"Right here?" he asked, knowing the answer.

"Yes!"

He gave the smallest of thrusts, and his shaft pierced her hole. She screamed his name and arched her ass higher. Creed let out a groan of his own. He had trouble not spilling his load with just that bit. She felt so good. Her body always gripped him like it would never let go, and he didn't mind at all.

"Damn it, Shada, you feel good."

"I want more," she whimpered.

"Easy. I'm not rushing this."

She reached for his wrist and gave it a tug. He resisted. Creed never let her control the rate at which they enjoyed sex, but he did all in his power to please her. Inch by inch, he sank into her, watching as his cock disappeared. Just seeing her body stretch around him, accommodating his thickness, set his teeth on edge and pulled at something buried in his core. He felt like any second he would explode and fill her with his come. That was impossible, of course, because he wore protection. That fact didn't stop him from imagining it and taking his desire for Shada to unheard-of levels.

Creed flattened both hands on the bed as he leaned over her and thrust forward. His cock sank to the hilt, and he withdrew until just the head pierced her ass. She wiggled her hips until he almost lost her, but he grabbed hold and ground in again. His mind blanked. Pleasure engulfed him.

He could hardly draw in a breath, but when he could, he claimed her. Over and over, he pounded deep, pulled back, and drove into her again. Shada cried out his name. She thrashed on the bed, pushed against him one minute and seemed to try to escape the next. Creed ran a hand beneath her and splayed his fingers over her belly. He brought his weight down on Shada and buried his dick as far as it would go. Leaning to the side, he watched as his crotch curved against her ass. They ground and plunged together, gasping and struggling. He loved the way their bodies moved in unison. Just seeing it turned him on, especially with the contrast in their sizes and even their skin tone.

Creed pumped into his lover and listened to the slap of their bodies coming together. The feel of her soft thighs against his prompted him to take her faster. He slid his hand down, from her belly to her pussy, and parted the lips to drive in two fingers. Hot wetness surrounded his digits. He squeezed her mound in his palm. She shuddered. He knew her body well enough to know she would come any second. Creed wrapped his other arm around her waist and let most of his weight come down on her. He rotated his hips to plow in and out of her ass. She screamed once and shook from head to toe. Just as he predicted, she came, her come dripping onto his hand.

When Shada was done, Creed took her with a few more pumps. Then he held his cock deep inside her. Seconds later, he emptied into the condom, imagining he'd lost his load in his sweet Shada. She made a small sound, and he pulled out, then rolled over. As he knew she would, she climbed onto his chest. He repositioned them both to lie the length of the bed. After he had discarded the used condom, he checked to be sure there were more.

Shada's drive matched his own, and they were far from done.

CHAPTER FOURTEEN

Creed stood in the kitchen, trying again to create a dish Shada might like. She'd eaten his sandwich and even said it was good, but he found himself questioning whether she'd said so because she was being kind. The doubt stirred his anger, but he swallowed it. This wasn't about him. She needed to eat, and he had to be sure she did. Simple as that.

When he carried the tray into the bedroom, it was just after eight in the morning. He had visited Marquette's the night before and bribed Rene into sharing a breakfast recipe or two with him. Today, he had made Shada an omelet with fresh lump crabmeat, finely chopped green onions, garlic, celery, and bell peppers. He had added salt and pepper to taste and cooked the whole in butter—"not margarine!"— as Rene instructed. Creed had decided to serve the omelet with a side of spicy breakfast potatoes and sour cream if Shada wanted it. He added a pot of coffee with cream and sugar.

With a smile on his face that refused to dim, he kicked the bedroom door wide and started inside. "I hope you're hungry, baby. I made—"

He stopped. Shada stood beside the bed, holding his cell phone and frowning down at the screen. She looked up at him. "I was groggy from the meds you gave me last night. When the phone started vibrating, I just assumed it was mine. I'd looked at it before I realized…"

She trailed off, but he knew there was more.

When he didn't speak, she held up the phone and turned the screen toward him. He couldn't see the words from so far away, but of course, he could guess what she'd found.

"You're still talking to her. I wasn't listening when you introduced her to everybody, but now I see her name is Madeline. She's the one you've chosen to have your baby, isn't she?"

"Shada, I didn't cheat."

She glared. "I didn't say you cheated, did I?"

He set the food tray down on the table in front of the settee. He'd liked this master bedroom from the moment he saw it, because of its size and the fact that he basically had a sitting room in his bedroom. He and Shada had never needed to leave this space except when he prepared food for them. Now he'd lost his appetite. "But you're angry."

She gave a dry laugh. "Who's angry? I asked you to fuck me. You did."

He grunted at the coarse words, knowing she'd chosen them on purpose. She wouldn't have said it the way she did if she weren't angry. "Shada."

"Shada, what? Is she pregnant yet?"

"Stop," he snapped. "We're not having this argument."

"Oh, because you control everything?"

"I'm not trying to."

"Yeah, right."

He approached her, his own anger rising. "I don't know what you're so pissed about. You turned me down, remember? Both for having my child and for being my lover."

"I said no because you thought you were going to have your cake and eat it too. Not with me you weren't."

The last of his patience evaporated. He snaked out a hand and jerked her to him. The move turned out to be a mistake, because his body lit on fire. Even angry at her, he wanted her. Maybe more. "You know it's not like that. If you looked at the texts, she was asking why she hadn't heard back from me after I brought her down here."

"You brought her…" Shada shook her head and thrust at his chest. "You were already seeing her in New York?"

"No. Well, not recently. We had a thing a couple years ago. I invited her down to New Orleans after you and I broke it off."

"But you introduced her to Damen and Stefan."

"I don't discuss my sex life with my brothers even though Damen tries to goad me into it. They hadn't met Madeline." He hesitated about how much to share, not wanting Shada to back off again. Something told him no matter what he said, this was a losing argument. "She wanted a closer relationship two years ago. I didn't. I think, rather I *thought*, she might be willing to change the dynamics this time around."

"And have your baby without having you."

He scratched the back of his head. Her blunt way of putting it made him sound like a self-serving ass. Maybe he was. "In a manner of speaking, yes."

Shada managed to get out of his arms. She held out his phone, and he took it. Then she spun away. "I'm leaving."

"Don't go. I made breakfast." He sounded like an idiot and cursed himself.

"It was a mistake coming here in the first place." She pulled on the black dress she'd worn to the funeral a few days ago. "I shouldn't have been leaning on you to get me through. I'm a strong woman. I can take care of myself."

"You know I don't mind."

She faced him, barefoot, no underwear on beneath her dress. Yet, his focus wasn't on getting her naked again. The night before, she had had another bout of tears, and he had held her until she stopped shaking. Then he had made love to her, *love* this time instead of raw, rough sex. They had both found pleasure in this method as well. What he most worried about was who would comfort her if she grew vulnerable again.

"Thank you for everything, Creed."

"You don't have to sound so damn formal."

"You're a good man in your way, a *really* good man."

Creed dropped his shoulders in resignation. His anger drained away. "We're not meant to be lovers or anything else."

A flash of something lit her gaze, but then she smiled a little, the first in days. "True."

He started to reach for her, and she went up to her toes, her hands rising as if they would wrap themselves around his neck. Then they both froze, and Creed took a step back. They couldn't kiss good-bye or risk her not going at all. He shoved fingers into his hair.

Shada spun away, gathered her panties and bra, and hooked a finger in the straps on her heels.

"I'll give you a ride home," he said.

"Thanks."

Creed drove her, both of them silent the entire way. At the street outside her apartment, he glanced over at her, but Shada was already reaching for the door to get out. He ground his teeth and turned back to face the street. The passenger-side door opened and closed. He slammed a fist into the steering wheel, and the horn blared. Creed threw the car into gear, and from the corner of his eye, he saw her turn around at the noise, but he kept going. Protests from other drivers lit the air at his sudden invasion into the traffic. Creed swerved to keep from being mowed down and headed toward Marquette's.

When he arrived at the restaurant, which was closed for the day, he used his key to let himself in. The wine cellar drew his steps, although even as he headed there, he wondered if he shouldn't go for something stronger. *One to shut out the noise and the images.*

Creed found a bottle of vodka and frowned at it. This would do the trick, he guessed, and he confiscated it to take to his office. Voices reached him as he walked down the hall, but he ignored them. When he opened the door to his office, he found Damen and Stefan there, and he swore. Stefan smiled and greeted him. Creed offered a grunt in response.

"Don't you two have homes?" he growled.

Damen's brows rose. He sat on the side of the desk, hands shoved into his pockets. Stefan stretched his long legs before the chair Creed usually occupied. They had discussed remodeling a couple of the other storage rooms into offices for his brothers but hadn't gotten around to it. Neither Damen nor Stefan liked to hang out in one long, which had always required him to chase them down in New York.

His middle brother's gaze lowered to the bottle in his hand, and Creed considered hiding it behind his back like a child. Instead, he frowned and stood taller. Damen's displeasure became obvious as he stood and approached Creed. By the time his brother reached him, all Creed could do was release the bottle as Damen took it.

"So you let her go," Damen said.

Creed tensed.

"I would have done anything," Damen said.

Creed opened his mouth to tell Damen this wasn't about him and how he handled his failed marriage, but Damen kept walking out the door with the vodka.

Stefan swung his feet to the floor, walked around the desk, and patted Creed's shoulder on his way out.

Creed moved to the window and stared out at the empty alley. He didn't stir for a long time, didn't think, and definitely didn't feel.

———

Creed set a hand at Madeline's lower back and pulled out her chair. She sank into it with graceful ease and crossed her long legs at the ankles. He noted the way her already short form-fitting dress rose higher and showed off sexy slender legs. Smooth and milky white, she didn't seem to have tanned yet beneath the Southern sun.

"Is there anything in particular you want to eat?" he asked as he perused the menu.

Madeline smiled and lowered her lashes. "You always did like to order for me."

He clenched his jaw. "You only have to say no for me to back off, Madeline."

"So sensitive." She tittered, a sound he had once found appealing.

Pull it together, Creed. This what you want.

They ordered, Creed choosing a random dish because food was the farthest from his mind tonight. He just wanted the preliminaries out of the way so he could get down to business. When the waiter had brought their order and Madeline had consumed about a third of her meal— her usual—he figured he didn't have to delay any longer. "I assume you accepted my invitation to come to New Orleans because you're not seeing anyone, or at least anyone serious?"

Pink tinged her cheeks. "Nope, not presently. Good timing."

He nodded and considered whether he should spend a few minutes trying to soften her up with compliments. Then again, why do that when he didn't feel it? He had never been misleading to a woman about his intentions and didn't want to start now.

"Madeline, I want you to have my baby."

Her jaw dropped, and her eyes widened. "You...?" She fanned her face, and the slight pink transformed into full-on red. "You're asking me to marry you?"

"No!"

"But you said you want me to have your baby." Some of the enthusiasm left her demeanor, but her eyes still twinkled.

Creed ignored the less than happy feeling in the pit of his stomach. He hadn't touched his food other than to shift the contents around the plate a few times. "I want a child, and I need a mother. It's as simple as that."

Madeline laughed, her tone full of disbelief. "You sound like one of these women who feel their eggs drying up and are desperate for kids."

She might not know it, but her words echoed Damen's. He resented the simile. "I'm not desperate. There is nothing wrong with wanting a child to carry on the Marquette name."

She smirked, for some reason reminding him of Shada. A longing started within him that could be termed "desperate," but he suppressed it. Madeline leaned forward and laid a willowy white hand over his. He wondered disjointedly if his enjoyment of her pale skin had gone because he'd experienced Shada's deep mocha. Perhaps he had developed a flavor for black women. The shallowness of that idea annoyed him.

"I'll do it," Madeline quipped.

He stiffened. "I haven't laid out the terms yet."

She winced. "Do you have to sound so businesslike, Creed? Honestly."

"This *is* business. I'm not asking you to have a relationship with me, Madeline. I need to make that clear from the start."

He caught the disappointment in her gaze and the tinge of hurt. "You didn't want a relationship two years ago, but you want a baby now."

"Yes, and I want to be honest with you."

Emotions flitted over her expressive face. "In vitro?"

"No, that's not necessary."

"Meaning you might as well enjoy yourself while you get what you want?" She preened. "Sure. Why not?"

"Don't you need to think about it? It's a big step to take, and there will be papers to sign."

That took her by surprise. "Papers?"

"I will require full custody."

"You've got to be kidding, Creed." He sat in silence, and she sighed. "Are you going to push to get me to sign over parental rights?"

"No, I wouldn't do that. The baby will know and love you as his or her mother."

"Thank you for small favors!"

"You are free to turn me down."

She glared at him. "I have loved you almost from the time I first laid eyes on you, Creed."

Guilt stirred in his gut. He shifted in his chair and drew away.

She swore. "Jeez, I see you're running away already. Always running away. I told myself to let you go two years ago, that anyone can see you're not the kind of man who will fall in love. Your parents ruined you."

He worked his jaw. "Don't psychoanalyze me, Madeline."

"Tell me it's not true," she demanded. "Have you ever come close to loving any woman? If you did, you wouldn't be sitting here across from me, asking me to have your baby and then wanting to have a contract drawn up to make it all nice and tidy."

"My corporation—"

"Bah! I neither need nor want your money, and you know it."

Creed couldn't argue. Madeline had spoken the truth. She commanded a six-figure income in her career as regional manager at a medium-sized corporation. In fact, that was how he met her, in the course of business. When they first became lovers, Damen had passed on what he'd learned of Madeline's background. Madeline had inherited a respectable sum from her maternal grandfather after he passed a few years before. So she was right. She didn't need his money. However, her assumption that he had never loved was wrong.

What the fuck? Where did that come from?

He cleared his throat and reordered his thoughts. "Why don't you think on it a little while longer? I'll call you in a few days."

She pushed out a thin bottom lip. "You're not going to comment on my confession?"

"Madeline—"

"Oh, forget it, Creed. I'll do it. Yes, I'm sure. I'm not getting any younger either, and in my line of work, most of the men I come across are already married. Most also don't mind a little playtime on the side, but none are going to offer me the chance to be a mother. So why not?"

Creed nodded. All of a sudden he was getting what he wanted, yet he questioned it. He had been thinking of having a child for a while now, and during the last few months in particular, about doing it this way. Why did it not appeal when Madeline said yes? He studied her flushed face as she searched her purse, and when she excused herself to visit the ladies' room, he watched her go. None of the emotions and the ache he'd experienced with Shada surfaced. In some ways, that was a good thing. This was the way it should be. He would control every aspect of the process before, during, and after. Every contingency would be planned until he held his son or daughter in his arms.

CHAPTER FIFTEEN

Creed stood against the wall on one side of his restaurant, observing the patrons. Or rather, he pretended to observe his guests. His attention had wandered to thoughts of Shada. She had been called from the kitchen countless times tonight, more often than Rene. He knew there would be some ruffled feathers to soothe later. Yet Shada's culinary creations were growing in popularity. He admitted he had allowed her free rein, and she used it to change up her offerings from week to week, sometimes night to night. Since they had separated and her sister had passed, she had thrown herself into her work. He knew in particular how that could help, and he hadn't stopped her.

Escorting her from the kitchen and introducing her to an honored guest usually fell to him. He had found it a challenge not to touch her or to stand so close the heat from her supple body ignited his. What he failed to do was keep his gaze off her. She had noticed, but she pointedly looked away each time she caught him looking.

"Creed." Madeline stepped into his line of vision, blocking out Shada. "Are you ready to go soon?" She practically radiated excitement, and he resented it.

"I told you I would pick you up," he snapped.

She pouted. "I was excited. This is our first night together."

He peered over her head. "We've been together before."

"Not this time around. I've been starving for your touch for two years."

He ground his teeth.

"What are you looking at?" she demanded and turned to follow his line of sight.

Too late, he realized he couldn't look away in time so she wouldn't know he stared at Shada.

Madeline frowned at his former lover and then glanced at him. "You want *her*? She's a cook, isn't she?"

"Forget it."

He elbowed past her and approached the table where Shada spoke with Arturo. As he drew nearer, he picked up snatches of their conversation, and it was definitely not about how good the food tasted. Creed moved to stand in front of Shada to block off Arturo. "She's not going anywhere with you."

Arturo offered a fake smile. "Come on, Creed. I'm not offering her a job. I promise."

Shada stepped out from behind him. "I don't need your protection, Creed. I've got this."

"You're on duty," he ground out. "Shouldn't you be in the kitchen?"

"I'm off early tonight. You should know. You drew up the schedule."

He looked into her eyes. They were duller than he remembered, and bags had formed beneath them. She wasn't sleeping enough.

He frowned in worry. "Well, then, you can get home earlier and get some rest."

She put her hands on her hips. "I don't think that's any of your business."

Arturo stood and reached for Shada's arm. "I was just waiting for her. We're going to catch a movie, if you must know."

Something snapped in Creed. "No. You're not."

Shada rounded on him. "Creed!"

In his head, he told himself to back off. She could see who she wanted, even this idiot who looked like all he wanted was to fuck her. Creed ground his teeth and reached for her arm. He drew her to him and thrust a hand in the middle of Arturo's chest. Somewhere he thought he saw a flash from a camera, but he couldn't be sure.

"You're making a scene," Shada complained, and she struggled in his hold. She leaned close and lowered her voice. "We're not together anymore, Creed. Let me go."

He was beyond listening. Creed glanced up and met Pete's eyes. A slight nod brought the man forward. Against Shada's protests, Creed drew her toward the kitchen. Madeline called out to him, but he picked up Damen's voice moments after as he spoke to her. Creed propelled Shada through the kitchen door and back toward his office.

She seemed to seethe all the way there, and when he released her, she took the opportunity to move to the opposite side of the room. "Well?" she demanded.

"Well, what?" He knew what she asked, but he had no words. Now that they were alone, he was ashamed of the way he had behaved, like a jealous boy. Words of apology refused to form on his lips.

"You manhandled me back here. To do what exactly, Creed? To tell me who I can and can't date?"

He frowned at her. "You know he's using you."

"So fucking what?"

He blinked at her.

"He wants to have sex. So do I."

"No!"

"Excuse me?"

He paced, cursing himself. Nothing calmed him. "I..." he began.

"I what?"

He had nothing.

She stomped toward the window, then stopped halfway there. Anger radiated off her in waves, and he didn't blame her. Irrational anger choked off his own words. He knew he had no right to behave the way he did.

"You don't want me, and you don't want anyone else to have me either. Is that it?" Her big brown eyes challenged him. He had a sudden urge to take her up on it.

One second, he stood near the door, the next, he crossed the floor in long strides to stand before her. He grasped her shoulders and pinned her to the wall, then aligned his body with hers. Her soft curves enticed him, her breasts so heavy and wonderful against his chest. He imagined her nipples hardening behind the white uniform she wore.

"Don't be foolish enough to think I don't want you," he ground out. "It's been two weeks since I've lain between your legs, and it feels like an eternity."

Her mouth dropped open.

He leaned back a little and raked her form with his gaze. A deep breath took in the scents so familiar about her, some of it evidence of the meals she had cooked and the rest Shada's own natural aroma. She drove him out of his mind, which was why he had lost it out there.

"W-we agreed," she stuttered.

"Yes, we agreed."

She licked her lips. Her gaze locked with his, and he swooped in close, enjoying her warm breath. He didn't allow a touch, though, or he would cross the line. How he longed to cross the line. *Then again, maybe I already have.* He almost uttered a delirious chuckle, positioned as he was with a hard-on pressed against her and Shada panting in obvious need.

"If we're not together..." she began.

"I can't watch you with someone else yet."

Her eyes widened at his admission. He had never felt so vulnerable with a woman, and he resented it. The words tumbled out of his damn mouth without him realizing he would make such confessions.

"Well, you made me watch."

He wasn't sure what she meant until he recalled Madeline showing up tonight in the restaurant, letting him know she was ready for their night together. Shada wouldn't have heard what Madeline said, but she must have assumed what it meant for the woman to be there.

"That wasn't my intention." He backed off, releasing her shoulders. Shada didn't move. His cock twitched, and he noted the tent in his pants. Damn, why couldn't he toss her over the desk and satisfy both their desires? "I told her I would pick her up."

"Well, I didn't expect to be asked out. I wasn't looking for it, but to tell you the truth, I wanted to get out of my own head. He provided an excuse."

An urge to go find Arturo and rip his head from his shoulders came over Creed. He stood still lest he follow through with the impulse. He wanted to shout like a caveman that she was his, and he would destroy any man who dared touch her. Why the hell did she do this to him? Was it just the sex? Couldn't he find another woman who would let him take her rough and obey his commands in that sex-kittenish way that Shada did? Of course, that must be it. Having Shada as his lover, he had developed a taste for an African American woman. The fire and heat might just be something to work out of his system, easily resolved with another woman.

Creed grinned, feeling much more charitable. He rearranged his cock in his pants and straightened his suit jacket. After he calmed, he spun to face her. "I apologize for behaving the way I did. Forgive me?"

She blinked at him.

For a moment, something stirred in his chest. He recalled his resolve.

Her lips parted. "Yeah, sure. Just don't let it happen again, or I'm gone. I love working here, but I'm not going to have you dictating my life, Creed."

He tensed and flared his nostrils.

She spread her fingers. "But I also know we didn't separate because the heat was gone. I won't accept any dates for a while at Marquette's. We can respect each other that much."

"Agreed."

She started toward him to pass by.

Creed fully intended to let her go. He had his plans, and they seemed logical in his mind. Somehow, whether he initiated it or she did, his fingers brushed hers. They lingered. The next instant, she was in his arms, her head tilted back, his hands cupping her jaw, and his mouth devouring hers. Creed told himself to stop and back off, but she chose that moment to arch into him, one of her hands coming up to squeeze his cock through his slacks.

He pleaded in silence for one or the other of them to gain strength. Yet his tongue delved deeper into her mouth, sweeping the warm recesses. When he managed to release her mouth, it was only to trail down the long column of her throat and taste the skin over a pounding pulse. She murmured his name, and he thrust everything on his desk to the floor, thumped her on top of it, and spread her legs. Shada lay back, and Creed rested a hand on her knee. All he could think of was getting her pants off and eating her delicious pussy. He knew she'd be wet and ready for him, and afterward, he'd sink his cock deep inside until she screamed his name.

"Wow, isn't this some kind of health violation?"

Creed sprang away from Shada, and she sat up to jump to her feet.

Damen stood in the doorway, smirking at the two of them. At Creed's scowl, he held up his hands and chuckled. "Dude, I just came to make sure she wasn't killing my big bro or something."

"You're not funny," Creed said and turned away to shift his cock again.

Shada muttered some excuse he didn't hear and pushed past his brother to escape. Creed could do nothing but watch her go. He'd crossed the line after all, but Shada had been right there with him. Thanking Damen for the interruption wasn't happening, but relief washed over him that his brother came in when he did. Needless to say, if Creed knew nothing else, he knew he would not be sleeping with Madeline tonight, or any other night. Now all he had to do was break the woman's heart, and he was horribly sorry he had fucked up so much that he needed to do it.

CHAPTER SIXTEEN

So," Arturo said, grinning at her from his side of her bed.

Shada's stomach churned, and she felt like she was going to throw up. Why the hell did she let him come to her apartment, and on top of that, why did she do it the same night she'd happily let Creed throw her on his desk and spread her legs like she was to be his Thanksgiving dinner?

The truth was she'd wanted to be. She'd wanted him to consume her and never stop until the need for him went away and he filled the hole Marisa left in her heart. She had said yes to Arturo because she hoped having his hands touch her body would erase all the bad stuff. Unlike when Creed touched her, she experienced the tiniest of sparks in terms of pleasure when Arturo kissed her. In fact, when his lips touched hers, she'd done all she could to pretend he excited her and raised her chin so he could move to her neck. How crazy was that? Why fake it? He didn't give her what she was looking for. Maybe no one could.

Except Creed.

No, Creed wasn't an option. He wanted a baby. She didn't. Opening her heart that wide wasn't possible. *No. Non. Nyet!*

"So," Arturo said again, "are you going to take off your clothes, or what?"

"I thought we were going to a movie."

He shrugged. "That's what I told Creed. You and I both know what we really want, don't we? I'm going to make love to you tenderly, like you want, and we'll both be satisfied."

"At what point did I tell you what I want?" She didn't mean to be snippy.

He grinned. "You're fiery too. I like that. How about I make it easy for you. I'll take my pants down, and all you have to do is get it hard and then ride it to your heart's content."

She could guess what he wanted her to do to get him hard. Her stomach churned again. She did not suck men's cocks the first time. She didn't even know this fool, and he had the boldness to ask for a blowjob.

Shada rolled away and stood up. As she strode toward the door, she rebuttoned her blouse. Arturo had gotten a peek at her breasts hidden behind her bra but nothing more. Let him ride himself. "This was a mistake," she called over her shoulder. "Please go."

"Wait, are you kidding me?" he growled. "You tease me all night, and I get the brush-off?"

She spun around at the door. "I don't know how I teased you all night from Marquette's kitchen."

"You know what I mean."

"No, I don't." She headed into the living room.

He followed, and she heard him stumbling, trying to put on his shoes, which he had kicked off on the way in.

The more she listened to him, the more irritated she grew and the more she wanted him gone. Trying to find a new lover two weeks after she had left Creed's bed was stupid, not to mention that they'd got all hot and heavy earlier tonight. She shivered in disgust comparing Creed's all-consuming, amazing kiss to Arturo's amateur hour.

Before she reached the door, Arturo grabbed her arm and spun her to face him. "It's because of him, isn't it? You're into him."

She feigned a yawn. "I don't know what you're talking about."

"Creed," he snapped. "Did you fuck him?"

"What I have and haven't done isn't your business."

"Yeah, you did."

He moved closer. She started calculating how likely it was she'd have to defend herself. Being from Brooklyn, she could handle herself to a certain extent.

"That's why he's so possessive of you," he spat. "Acts like he owns you."

She shrugged, pretending it didn't matter. "Maybe I own him. He could be my little pet, you know, like dominatrix stuff." Her mind had totally gone out to lunch, she decided. Where was all this coming from?

At her words, Arturo's eyes widened, and he seemed too

interested in what she claimed. Then a new thought struck her. Arturo might be that type. This wouldn't be the first time her mouthy attitude gave the impression she liked to discipline men. The thought alone grossed her out.

"So you like those kind of games, huh? I guess I don't blame him for getting too attached." Arturo grabbed for her wrist and laid the other hand at her waist.

She decided he'd gone too far and kneed him as hard as she could in the balls. He yelped in pain and doubled over.

Shada stepped back and raised her fists. While she had a good stance and could do more damage, Arturo was thick-set. If he chose to, he could hurt her bad. Her belly did flip-flops. On the other hand, she wouldn't go down without a fight.

"I said get out," she repeated, "or I'll lodge your balls in your throat with my next kick."

She thought he would take the hint. She *prayed* he would.

"You dirty bitch!"

He lunged at her. She ducked, hit the floor, and rolled to the side. He caught her ankle and dragged her back. Shada screeched and started to kick backward, but his grip was a vice that hurt like hell. The pain lasted only a moment, because both of them were distracted by the *boom* of her front door exploding inward and slamming against the wall.

Arturo lost his grip on her ankle as Creed's bodyguard filled the doorway. He stepped aside, and Creed charged across the room to snatch up Arturo by his collar. A well-placed fist sent her attacker to the floor, but Creed dragged him up just to smash his nose a second time. "You dare fucking touch her, you piece of shit?" he roared.

Creed reared back to punch Arturo again, and even Shada started to feel sorry for the man, with his blood gushing everywhere and his head bobbling about his neck.

Pete caught Creed's arm midswing and didn't even struggle much against Creed's momentum. "He's had enough."

Creed looked like he was about to round on the bodyguard for daring to tell him anything, but he dropped Arturo and rushed to Shada. She found herself lifted in a tender embrace and carried to the couch.

She pushed at Creed's chest when he sat down with her on his lap. "I'm fine, Creed. I was taking care of it."

"You screamed," he complained. "That's taking care of it?"

"It was more like a yelp."

The fact that her teeth chattered from the rush of adrenaline did nothing to help her case.

Creed frowned at her and proceeded to examine her from head to toe.

She slapped at his hands to no avail, but it did feel good for him to come to her defense. "I have to thank your bodyguard for breaking down my door."

From the sour expression on his face, Creed didn't like that. "He rushed ahead of me, or I would have done it myself. The man takes his job too damn seriously."

She chuckled. With each second he was there, she began to calm down more and more. Unable to help it, she lay on his shoulder and shut her eyes. A single tear rolled down her cheek, and Creed stroked her back. Not even the sounds of the bodyguard helping Arturo out the door and then shutting the broken thing awkwardly could make her lift her head.

"What are you doing here?" she mumbled into Creed's chest.

"I came for you."

She sat up. "What do you mean?"

"I'm not going to have a child."

She gasped. "What? Creed, you can't do that. You've always wanted a baby."

"Only in the last year or two." He shrugged, but she knew it was a huge desire to let go. "I asked a woman out tonight, a black woman."

Jealousy reared up inside her, but she chewed the inside of her cheek to keep silent.

"She was beautiful and sexy. I knew with a bit of prompting I could get her into bed."

"But?" She found herself hoping the woman turned out to be a man or that she had a wooden leg, was bald-headed, and dumb as a stump.

"She wasn't you."

Her chest constricted. "Me?"

Creed pushed a hand into her hair, half cupping her cheek. "You, Shada. Damen has been trying for weeks to get me to face up to how I feel. It's got to be you. I'm not asking you to love me... No, I *am* asking, but I'm willing to wait. I love you right now, today. I never thought it was possible, but I do. I want to be with you so badly, and if it means I have to give up my dream of a child to have you, then I'll do it."

"Creed." She started crying in earnest. "You can't do that. I don't want to be selfish. You deserve a cute little mini-Creed running around."

He chuckled and kissed her lips. A fire ignited in her belly and spread to her pussy. His hand lay on her hip, but she craved it between her legs. Creed massaged the area where his palm rested, stirring her desires higher. He released her lips and touched his forehead to hers.

"Whether I deserve a child or not, or if I will ever have one, right after your loss is not the time to even discuss it."

She acknowledged that was true.

"What I do know is how I feel about you."

He waited for her to speak, and she ducked her head, pushing into his chest again. How could she say what he had? Admit to him and herself that she loved him? She had promised herself she would never love anyone again. Sure, everyone went through loss, and most recovered. Logic said this was true, but fear closed her throat and stole her words. She shivered and tried hard to pull herself together, but the more she tried, the more scattered her emotions seemed.

Creed raised her up in his arms and carried her toward the bedroom.

"The door," she protested.

"He'll keep watch until we can get someone out here to fix it in the morning."

"That's unfair."

Creed set her gently on the bed and knelt down before her. His hands moved toward her pants to undo the button, but he stopped and looked into her face. "Do you at least accept me as your lover?"

Her heart hurt. "Yes."

"I want to make it clear," he said. "I'm not going to sleep with anyone but you, and no other man gets to touch you."

She grinned. "Do I get to kick your door in and beat her up if you try?"

He chuckled. "If you think you can."

She smacked his shoulder, but he moved over her like a predator, eyes narrowed. Shada lay back and slid up the bed. Creed followed. He paused, hovering over her, and the expression on his face changed. She had never seen him look so tender toward anyone, but for the first time she saw the love he professed reflected in his eyes. Her heart raced. She found it hard to breathe.

He ran gentle fingertips along her face, down to her collarbone and lower, to her breast. "Shh," he whispered.

A soft squeeze sent a pulse through her pussy. She squirmed and lowered her eyelids.

He called out her name, and she looked up at him.

"I'm not going easy."

The look in his eyes contradicted his words, but she believed him. Shada didn't want coddling. She waited for him to shed every stitch of her clothing. When he finished, he reared back to remove his clothing as well, his gaze never leaving her body. She watched as his cock rose, tight and hard, straining in her direction. She licked her lips.

Creed focused on her ankle and brushed a thumb over the one that Arturo had grabbed. She hadn't bruised, and any pain she experienced was long gone. Still, a flash of anger surfaced in Creed's eyes, and then it was gone. He moved to the side of the bed and faced away from her. A pat on his lap brought her to him, and she lay down across his lap. Anticipation made her arch and raise her hips. Her pussy gushed at the first smack to her ass cheeks.

"Creed," she moaned.

"You've been a very naughty girl, Shada." Another sharp smack. "Taking this beautiful body from me."

"Yes." She wiggled in his hold, her breasts crushed against his hard thigh. "I deserve a good, hard spanking."

"Or two," he said.

His hand rose and fell a half-dozen times, and she begged for more. He spanked her again, and her lust blazed white-hot. She dug her nails in his thigh, holding on and squirming. Creed landed the last smack and leaned down to kiss her ass cheeks. He gave them a gentle lick and stilled. Eyes shut, she lay panting.

"You need to come," he said. The words weren't a question, but a reflection of his intimate knowledge of her body. All he had to do was reach under her and touch her throbbing center. A convulsion of muscle, and seconds after his fingers sank into her heat, she came, screaming his name.

Creed flipped her over and tossed her onto the bed. He spread her legs and buried his mouth between them. His noisy laving at her wetness set her off again, and she moaned through the aftershock of an orgasm that seemed as strong as the first. When her lover raised his head, she marveled at the moisture on his face. He ran a hand over it and licked away any excess.

How long could she keep a man like Creed? He was so wild and strong, so full of life. Forever wouldn't be enough, but an instant, what about that? "Creed, I—"

"Shh," he whispered a second time. He moved above her and guided her legs around his waist. With one violent thrust, he plunged his cock inside her. *So cruel and wonderful, all at the same time.* She closed her eyes and encircled his neck with her arms. Creed drew back and pushed in again. Her pussy walls gave way to the invasion. He lifted one of her thighs high enough to bring her ass up off the bed, and he spanked it once. She shook with pleasure. Then he began a slow and easy stroke, in and out. When she didn't think she could hold on any longer, he picked up the pace, pounding into her, guiding his cock so he didn't cause damage but just enough of an ache to drive her crazy. His throaty growl in her ear let her know he loved the sensations, and in the next instant, he emptied himself inside her.

After some time, Creed sat up. He raised both her legs and pushed them against her chest. Quiet, he stared at her pussy. She looked down to find they were both so wet. His cock glistened with a mingling of their juices. He guided his shaft forward and back over her slit, never looking away. She moaned each time the head touched her clit. While they both watched, he grew hard again. Creed directed his slick shaft farther back and let the tip touch her ass opening. She caught her bottom lip between her teeth.

His gaze met hers. He waited a beat. Then he pushed in, slow and easy. Shada couldn't keep her eyes open. In fact, she couldn't do anything other than lay there and let her man pleasure her. He thumped his dick deep inside her ass and pulled all the way out. Somehow he got off on popping it past her barrier. Going slow until her muscles relaxed a little more, he sped up when she was ready. Their bodies banged together over and over. Being deeper in the back, she could take all of Creed, and he could pump faster and harder.

She scratched at the sheets as he ravaged her hole, giving her pleasure until she couldn't take it anymore.

"Look at me," he demanded.

She met his gaze, and they stared at each other as he reached his release.

After a long and satisfying session, Creed pulled out of her body and rose. He held out his hand, and she took it to join him. They stood in the shower moments later, allowing the warm water to cascade over their heads. Her hair would be a royal mess in the morning, but she didn't care.

When they were clean, Shada snagged towels for them and handed one to Creed. He tossed his aside and snatched her into his arms. With purposeful movements, he dried her off and cocooned her in the towel. After she was done, he worked on himself.

"Are you hungry?" she asked. "I'll make you something to eat."

"No. I just want you here." He pointed to his chest.

She grinned, and they strode hand in hand back to the bedroom. "Um, wow, those sheets are pretty gross."

"Whose fault is that?" he quipped.

"Yours. I guess you didn't notice me on my tiptoes."

"I noticed and felt proud of myself."

"Bum!"

He tapped her ass with a soft palm. "Well, we could change them now or get them dirtier."

She shook her head. "You're impossible. You know that?"

His eyes twinkled. In the end, they changed the sheets, dressed, and headed to the kitchen for her to cook for him and his bodyguard. After she made up the couch for Pete, she and Creed returned to the bedroom, and she spent the rest of the night folded in his arms.

———

"More compliments to the chefs," Tiffany called to Rene when she banged through the door.

Rene nodded his acknowledgement, pink tingeing his cheeks. Shada smiled. She had to admit it was nice to be back in the restaurant. The few days she had taken off, with Creed caring for her after Marisa's death, had been needed, but after she had gone back to her own apartment and threw herself into her work, what she loved soothed her. She recalled the many times Marisa had chirped over a new dish and told Shada this was her calling. Marisa had convinced her to go after what she loved, and doing so made Shada feel like she made her sister happy in heaven. Thinking that way eased the pain a little more every day.

Not to mention Creed's touch and the way he looks at me.

Thinking of the devil brought him through the door, and her heartbeat sped up.

He raised dark brows in question. "I believe the compliments were to the chefs, plural? The mayor and his party are waiting."

Shada rolled her eyes. "He's been here fifty times."

"Yes, but this is a new set of 'friends' that need to be impressed with who he knows."

Shada removed her apron. "A chef?"

"The chefs of the famous billionaire restaurant owners," Stefan announced when he walked in on the tail end of the conversation. He grinned, too pleased with himself, apparently. "We were featured in an article recently. Not so flattering for hothead over here, but great exposure nonetheless."

Shada had seen the article, a write-up of Marquette's, exposing them to a broader audience and coupled with a picture of Creed squaring off against Arturo. The picture pissed Creed off, made Shada laugh, and had Stefan declaring they were just about where he envisioned them to be, whatever that meant.

"Are you coming?" Creed asked, holding out his hand.

"We can't go out there holding hands, Creed."

Amusement filled his eyes, but he conceded, and she started ahead of him. His presence behind her bolstered her and made her feel loved and cared for. She paused at the door before pushing through, and she looked back at him.

Confusion clouded his beautiful eyes. "Is something wrong?"

She swallowed. "I just wanted to say…I love you too."

THE END

ABOUT THE AUTHOR

Tressie Lockwood is the national bestselling author of interracial erotic romance. She has always loved books, and she enjoys writing about heroines who are overcoming the trials of life. She writes straight from her heart, reaching out to those who find it hard to be completely themselves no matter what anyone else thinks. She hopes her readers enjoy her stories.

Visit Tressie on the web at www.tressielockwood.com or on her blog at tressielockwood.blogspot.com.

Made in the USA
San Bernardino, CA
14 September 2015